The black rock was both slippery and jagged as I struggled to pull myself up onto the ledge. I felt skin tearing but didn't care. As long as I could rest with my head out of the water, I'd be okay. I hoped. I wasn't really sure. I just knew I needed to get out of the lake.

When I found a crack in the rock and dug my fingers into it, I used every ounce of strength I had to position myself. With a great heaving sob, I draped myself across the uneven slab, my feet still dangling in the water. I lay there listening to my heart pound in my head. My mouth was dry, my tongue thick. I tried to look at my leg to see the wound, but my vision blurred as quickly as my ability to speak. Had I been stung by something poisonous? A fresh-water jellyfish? Was there such a thing? I couldn't make my mind work clearly.

Suddenly, something pierced through the numbness in my ankle. It felt like someone tickling me with barbed wire. I wanted to turn my head to see what was causing this new sensation, but my neck wouldn't budge. My eyes were open, but I could only see what was right in front of me, and even that was fuzzy. My fingers dug into the rock, frantically clinging for safety, but with a terror I hadn't felt before, I realized I was being pulled back down into the water.

4th Down

A CASSIDY JAMES MYSTERY

BY
KATE CALLOWAY

THE NAIAD PRESS, INC.
1998

Printed in the United States of America on acid-free paper
First Edition

Editor: Christine Cassidy
Cover designer: Bonnie Liss (Phoenix Graphics)
Typesetter: Sandi Stancil

Library of Congress Cataloging-in-Publication Data

Calloway, Kate, 1957 –
    Fourth down : a Cassidy James mystery / by Kate Calloway.
        p.   cm.
    ISBN 1-56280-193-7 (pbk.)
    I. Title.
PS3553.A4245F68   1998
813'.54—dc21   97-40430
                                                               CIP

For Carol,
The love of my life

Acknowledgments

A heartfelt thanks to my friends (again!) for taking the time to read and critique a work in progress: Murrell, Linda, Carolyn, Lyn, Deva, and especially Carol who keeps me honest! Thanks, too, to Christi Cassidy for her encouragement and unerring eye, and to all my friends and family for their continued support. Finally, thanks to those readers who have offered such kind feedback and support in their letters, reviews and notes on the Internet. Believe me, it's appreciated.

About the Author

Kate Calloway was born in 1957. She has published several novels with Naiad including *First Impressions, Second Fiddle,* and *Third Degree,* all in the Cassidy James Mystery Series. Her short stories appear in the Naiad Press anthologies *Lady Be Good* and *Dancing in the Dark.* Her hobbies include cooking, wine-tasting, boating, song-writing and spending time with Carol. They split their time between Southern California and the Pacific Northwest, setting for the Cassidy James novels. Those who know Kate well say that Cassidy James is not entirely fictional.

Chapter One

The hand around my ankle tugged me downward, into the murky depths of the lake. My lungs were close to bursting and my eyes strained in the black water as I struggled to see the shimmering light of day above. If only I could somehow break free. But the grip was fierce, and no matter how hard I kicked against the evil thing, it held tight. My ears had started to ring and I felt myself losing consciousness.

"Cass, it's for you. Come on, wake up, Cass. You're having another dream."

Maggie's voice drifted toward me like a thread of

hope and I found myself gulping for air as I blinked awake. I looked at her blankly.

"Same dream?" she asked. I nodded, shaking off the dread that had threatened to engulf me. This made the third time in a week that I'd dreamed of something dark and evil pulling me down, holding me under. Worst of all, it felt like a premonition. Maggie was holding the phone in one hand, rubbing my shoulder with the other. "You want me to tell them to call back?" She was propped up on one elbow, leaning over me, her breasts partially exposed above the sheet.

"Whoizzit?" I managed. My heart still pounded erratically from the dream and my mouth wasn't working.

"Didn't say. Sounds worried." Maggie's voice had a sexy morning quality to it — husky and deep. She held the receiver above my head, smiling seductively. "Yes or no?"

She knew I hated being awakened from dreams, especially by the phone. While I debated, she pulled the sheet up across her breasts, leaving just the tip of one nipple exposed. I moaned and sat up to take the receiver.

"Cassidy James?"

"Speaking." Barely.

"This is Allison Crane. I wonder if I might come out there right away. I've rented a boat. I just need directions."

"Right now?" I glanced at the clock. It was not quite eight. On Sunday morning.

"If it's too early, I can wait. The thing is, time is somewhat of the essence."

"And this is regarding?" I let it hang.

"I'm in need of your professional services. Martha Harper gave me your name. She says you're good. And honest. And discreet. That's what I need."

Martha Harper was my best friend and not entirely objective.

I said, "Well, since you're already here, I suppose we could at least talk." I gave her directions and handed the phone back to Maggie who was nuzzling my ear. "Another of Martha's referrals," I sank back into the pillow. "She's on her way."

"I need to get going anyhow," Maggie said, pulling away.

"You don't need to leave," I argued. "Stay. I'll make you Belgian waffles."

"Cass, if I continue to let you cook for me, I'm going to have to buy an entire new wardrobe. Besides, I have more to do today than I can handle. Really."

Reluctantly, I agreed. I watched as she slipped into form-fitting slacks and a silky, button-down blouse. I marveled at the way my heart still skipped when I looked at her. With black curly hair, olive skin and sea-green eyes, she was muscular but full of curves.

"I don't suppose I could just meet with her in here," I said, stretching out across the bed.

"Over my dead body." She tossed me my shirt and headed for the bathroom. With a sigh, I forced myself out of bed and got dressed.

When I walked Maggie down to the dock, the August sky was speckled with white puffy clouds, but it looked like the recent rain was over. The water was glassy with hardly a ripple along the surface.

"Do you have a client today?" Maggie was a

3

therapist, and I knew she sometimes met with her clients on Sundays, but only if they were really desperate. Otherwise, their bruised and battered psyches would have to wait until Monday. Usually, she kept her weekends free for us.

"No client. I have some errands to run, and I want to work in the garden. Plus I'm making something special."

I looked at her quizzically, holding the bowline while she climbed into the little dinghy. She smiled mysteriously.

"For next Sunday," she said. She yanked the pull-rope fiercely and the outboard coughed to life. Smiling, I watched her ease away from the dock. I'd been wondering if she'd remember. Next Sunday was our one-year anniversary.

Of course, the year hadn't exactly been what one would call smooth sailing. No sooner had I met Maggie than my previous lover, Erica Trinidad, waltzed back into my life. No matter how much I tried to convince her that I was no longer interested in Erica, Maggie suspected otherwise. And then like a jerk, I actually admitted that I did in fact still have feelings for Erica. I not only admitted it, I acted on them. *Jerk* didn't begin to describe it. Luckily, all that was behind us.

Despite these inauspicious beginnings, Maggie and I had begun to develop a deeply satisfying relationship. It wasn't just the mutual attraction; we really liked each other. We connected on an emotional level and also shared a somewhat perverse sense of humor. Most of all, we had fun. And she kept me on my toes. If there was one drawback, it was that Maggie

4

tended to be jealous. But then, considering my behavior with Erica, who could blame her?

I'd been racking my brains for weeks, trying to think of the perfect anniversary gift, but still hadn't been able to decide. Now, I had less than a week to figure it out.

Panic and Gammon joined me on the dock and were busy sniffing the various hoof and paw prints in the mud along the bank. It looked like our most recent visitors had included a doe and its fawn, along with a large raccoon. The cats themselves looked like wild animals. Part Bengal, part Egyptian Mau, they were spotted instead of striped, with large pointed ears and gooseberry eyes. Gammon was on the portly side, while Panic was as lithe as a ferret. When an outboard rounded the island across from us, Panic bounded up the bank toward safety. Gammon just crouched down on the dock, tail twitching, watching me expectantly.

"It's just a client," I told her. "Nothing to get excited about."

But as the little rental boat scooted across the water toward my dock, I was feeling a little on-edge myself. Probably just that damned dream I kept having, I thought, watching the boat approach. She was coming in straight enough, but a bit too fast for a novice. I waved, letting her know she had the right dock and she waved back. Maybe she knows her way around boats, I thought. Nearing the dock, she suddenly turned the handle the wrong way and goosed the motor. The nose of the aluminum boat rammed the dock and she flew forward, landing in the middle of the boat on all fours. I leaped in, cut the motor and grabbed onto the side of the dock to steady us. Slowly, she got up, her face crimson.

"You okay?" I asked.

She nodded, looking mortified. "Sorry. I've never actually driven one of these before. I can handle a sailboat. I thought this would be easy. I hope I didn't damage your dock."

"No problem." I hopped out and secured the boat to a metal cleat. Somewhat awkwardly, she scrambled out behind me.

"Allison Crane," she said, extending a pale, lightly freckled hand.

I was surprised at the strength of her grip, given her delicate features and I studied her more closely. Her short hair was a blend of red and gold, tossed in careless waves around her face. Her eyes were almost turquoise, the color of the Caribbean. Her skin was milky and smooth, with a splash of freckles across her nose that made her seem vulnerable. When she smiled, two tiny dimples appeared on her cheeks. Allison Crane, I decided, was an attractive woman.

"Come on up. I'll put on some coffee." I led her up the walkway to my house, wishing I had taken the time to make myself more presentable. I was wearing jeans and an old sweatshirt, and though I'd run a comb through my short blond hair and brushed my teeth, I wasn't exactly dressed for company. But then, she hadn't given me a lot of warning. Even so, I found myself checking my reflection in the entryway, self-consciously smoothing my hair.

Chapter Two

"Someone's trying to kill me," she stated, sipping her coffee. Her tone was calm and matter-of-fact.

"How?" I'd started to ask her how she knew, but thought better of it. She didn't seem like the kind of person who'd imagine these things.

"In the last three weeks there have been three separate attempts on my life. The first one happened in my office, at Women On Top."

"You work with Women On Top? The group that sponsors the dances?"

She laughed. "We do a lot more than that. The

dances, golf tournaments and concerts are primarily fund-raisers for our real work which is to help lesbians succeed in the business world. We provide scholarships, sponsor networking seminars, and host conferences. We help small businesses secure start-up loans and apply for grants. Our headquarters are in Portland, but we have chapters in cities across the country." Her face was flushed with pride and she smiled apologetically. "Forgive me. I get passionate about this. I'm the president."

I was momentarily taken back. "Is that a paid position?"

"Well, we're basically volunteers, though the amount of time the staff puts in certainly warrants a regular salary. A year ago we voted to pay the officers a nominal fee, though it doesn't amount to much. It's become a sore point with some of us. But if we use our funds to pay ourselves, it takes money away from our goals." She shrugged.

"What do you do for a living, then?"

"I'm an M.D. I work at a women's clinic in Portland." If she was trying to impress me with her credentials, she was succeeding. But she seemed oblivious to this fact.

"So, you think someone tried to kill you at Women On Top?"

She nodded. "You see, I'm allergic to bee stings," she said, as if this explained everything. I waited, hoping I'd catch on. "About three weeks ago, I came into the office around six, which I often do on Saturday mornings, before anyone else is there. I like to make the coffee, get things organized for the day, you know. Once the others arrive, it tends to get chaotic." She shrugged. "Anyway, I noticed right away that the

8

door to my office was closed, which was unusual, but I didn't give it any real thought. I just turned the knob and pushed the door open. That's when I heard them. There must've been a thousand bees inside. They buzzed around like they were really agitated. I was almost through the door when I realized what I was hearing. You know how little time it takes to open a door and walk into a room?" Her aqua eyes widened, willing me to imagine her predicament. "Another step or two and I'd have been covered with them. As it was, I jumped back and slammed the door before I got stung."

"Did you call the police?"

"Yes. Immediately. I figured it was some kind of hate crime. You know, Homophobes Against Lesbos, or some damned thing. We receive quite a bit of hate mail. The officer who came out wasn't much help. I don't think he took the whole thing very seriously. It never occurred to me that the attack was personal. Until the next one. That's when I really started to get scared."

"Wait. How did they get the bees inside?" I asked, tasting my coffee for the first time.

"The police said that someone must've left a window open. We're on the ground floor so all they had to do was toss in the bee box from the outside and close the window. The last person to leave always sets the alarm, so it had to be done while people were still working inside Friday night."

"Can just anybody enter your office? You said your door was closed, and that you usually leave it open."

"I was there Friday evening until about seven. So were half a dozen others. I left my door open as usual when I left. I asked around later, and no one remembers anyone else going in there after I left. So maybe someone who has a key to our building came in later. That's why I think it's someone from Women On Top. In fact, I know it is. I just don't know who."

"You think someone in your own organization is trying to kill you?"

Her blue-green eyes were suddenly wet and shiny. She nodded, biting her lip. "I found a piece of paper on my desk the next day. There were just two words typed in the center — *First Down*. I didn't have a clue what it meant and it didn't really click until the second attempt. That's when I realized it was someone I knew." She paused and took a sip of coffee. "I live on a steep hill and my driveway is quite long. At the bottom of the drive, there's an intersection to a major thoroughfare and the cars whiz by at fifty or sixty miles an hour. Usually, I just coast down the drive, hit the brakes and wait for a clearing. Even so, I usually have to gun it. Luckily the Porsche accelerates quickly. I wouldn't want to pull out into that traffic in a VW."

I chuckled.

"Anyway, last Friday I got a call that there was an emergency at the hospital. It was just after five, the rush hour. I jumped in the car and sped a little faster than usual down the driveway. When I hit the brakes at the bottom, nothing happened. Someone had cut my brake lines. I just kept on rolling straight across four lanes of traffic. That I'm still alive is a miracle. Cars were swerving all over the place but not one of them so much as dented a fender. When I finally came to a stop, I did something I haven't done in years."

I arched my eyebrows and she smiled self-consciously.

"I prayed," she said. She ran her fingers through her red-gold curls and watched my reaction.

"What did the police say? Are you positive that your brakes were actually cut?"

"I had the car towed to my mechanic. He's the one who told me what had been done. The police said they would look into it. I told them about the bee incident and they took down the information but I still don't think they were all that concerned. They treated it more like a prank than a serious attempt on my life."

"Anybody in your group know a lot about cars?" I asked. Personally, I wasn't sure I'd be able to recognize a brake line if I saw one.

Allison nodded. "That's the first thing I thought of. Reeva Dunsmoore's a mechanic. And she, more than anyone, has reason to want me out of the picture. She's my vice-president and doesn't hesitate to let people know she'd do things differently if she were in my position. She's one of the people who think we should be getting paid more. She's also big on football."

I raised a brow.

"The morning after my brakes were cut I found another note on my desk with the words *Second Down* typed on the front. Believe me, the first person I thought of was Reeva. But now, I don't think it's her — not because I totally trust her, but because whoever made the third attempt had to be someone who's been in my home, who knows my daily routine. Reeva and I have never been that close. I don't think it could've been her."

Panic and Gammon had come back into the house and were busy sniffing Allison's shoes. Apparently Gammon found them to her liking because uninvited, she leaped onto Allison's lap and began kneading her thighs.

"My God, what do you feed this cat? She must weigh twenty pounds!" she said as she started to stroke her silky fur.

"It's just her metabolism. She doesn't eat any more than her sister. Luck of the draw, I guess." I got up and poured us more coffee. "What was this third attempt and what makes you think it was by someone who knows your routine?"

"I guess I'm a creature of habit," she said, shifting Gammon on her lap. "Every morning I have the same thing for breakfast — a bowl of cereal and a glass of orange juice. Not very exciting, but it's quick and easy. It's not something I've ever discussed with anyone, but anyone who's spent the night more than once would probably have noticed.

"On Wednesday morning I got a call from the hospital before I got a chance to eat my cereal. Unlike the Friday before, this call really was from the hospital. I'd found out that whoever called the night my brakes were cut just pretended to be from the nurse's station, so I was being cautious. The emergency this time was legitimate so I rushed out without even taking time to put my cereal bowl in the fridge. If I had, Susan B. Anthony might still be alive today."

"I beg your pardon?" Her eyes had filled up with

12

tears and I thought briefly that this one might be a real nut case.

She smiled sadly. "My blue-point Siamese, Susan B. Anthony. I'd had her almost twelve years. The poor thing jumped up on the table and helped herself to the milk in my bowl. I found her on the living room floor." The tears that had welled up now trickled down her cheeks and I felt a lump in my throat. It took her several moments to compose herself, and when she finally spoke, her voice was thick with emotion. "I'm sorry. You have no idea how much I loved that old cat. And I know she suffered. I'm not just scared anymore, I'm furious." Indeed her cheeks had taken on a high color and her eyes shone with little green specks of light.

"You think someone broke into your house and poisoned your milk, knowing that you'd have it with your cereal? And that's why you think it must be someone who knows your habits?"

She nodded, biting her lip. Gammon, always good at sensing grief, burrowed her head into Allison's chest and began purring loudly. Allison handed me a piece of plain typing paper with the words *Third Down* printed in the center. The print was laser-quality and could've been generated from any standard computer. Which was too bad, I thought. A typewriter would have been easier to trace.

"I took the milk to the police and they said they'd run tests on it but I was worried that things were happening too fast. I might be dead by the time they got around to looking into it. I'd met Martha Harper during a fundraiser a few years ago and we've run into each other a few times since. She's the only cop I really know, so I called her, even though she's all the way out here in Kings Harbor. I knew she couldn't do much good from here while I'm in Portland, but I didn't know where else to turn."

"And she suggested me," I said.

Allison nodded. "She said you were her best friend, that she'd known you since college and that you were someone to trust."

"I'm not sure I'd be much help —"

She cut me off. "But I've got a plan! Please don't say no until you've heard me out. I've thought it through and I know it could work. Will you at least listen?"

I nodded, my curiosity getting the better of me.

"Next week, everyone on my staff will be going on a week-long retreat, along with about a hundred other lesbians. Maybe you've heard about it? It's this big corporate retreat outside of Portland called Eagle's Nest, and once a year we rent the place. A lot of people look at it as a vacation, but it's also a place for networking and tapping mutual resources. We sponsor workshops and team building activities throughout the week. Not that it's all work and no play. You should see the waiting list to get in. Anyway, I think it's a logical assumption that whoever is trying to kill me will try again there." She paused and added wryly, "They're running out of downs. Or I am."

"If I were you, I'd consider skipping the retreat this year."

"And spend the rest of my life looking over my shoulder?" Her eyes flashed anger. "Listen. Everyone I work with will be right there. I'm certain that whoever is doing this will try again. With you there

14

watching, maybe we can catch her. Before she succeeds."

"What?" The tone of my voice frightened the cats. Gammon jumped down from Allison's lap.

"Don't you see? No one knows you're a private investigator. You'll be just another businesswoman at the retreat. We can pretend to meet the first night and hit it off. While everyone thinks you only have eyes for me, you'll really be keeping your eye on them. That way, you can interact with my inner circle without raising suspicions."

"You want me to pose as your girlfriend?" My expression must have shown more than I intended.

She laughed. "Is that such a horrible notion?"

"No, I didn't mean that." For some reason, I found myself blushing. "It's just that, I mean, I've never worked undercover before." It sounded pretty lame and I knew it.

"You *are* a private investigator?" She was daring me to turn her down.

"Well, yeah, but . . . I don't know. This seems like something the police should be handling."

"That's what Martha said. But then she came up with this, and I think it just might work."

"This was Martha's idea?" I was going to kill her. She was forever getting me in over my head.

"Well, we sort of thought it up together. It could work, don't you think?" She went on quickly before I could answer. "And even if it doesn't, what other choice do I have? I don't think they're going to give up easily. I'd feel better just knowing someone was watching out for me. I mean, if you decide to take the case, that is. As it is, I haven't slept in weeks."

It was true her eyes were ringed with dark circles. My mind was racing, trying to think of some reason why I couldn't accept this case, but the truth was, it wasn't a bad plan. If in fact her would-be murderess worked for Women On Top, then it was likely that she'd try again at the retreat.

"Why are you so sure that it has to be someone from the office? I mean, aside from the bees and those notes, there doesn't seem to be any connection. What about family members, lovers, co-workers at the hospital?"

"Women On Top *is* my family. Period." She looked up, daring me to challenge this assertion. When I said nothing, she went on. "As for lovers, well, that's why I suspect it's someone on my staff. Between my private practice and my work in the organization, I don't have much time for a private life. But that doesn't mean I want to live a life of celibacy. I've always been upfront with the women in my life about just how much time and energy I'll be able to give them. Over the years, I've dated a few of the women I work with. That's what makes this so difficult. Not only are these women my friends, quite a few of them have been my lovers."

Her gaze held mine, challenging me once again to find fault with this admission. She was an intriguing woman, I thought. Vulnerable one second, intensely direct the next.

"I'll need to know which ones," I said.

"I made a list." She dug in her purse and I thought I detected a faint blush, which was gone by the time she handed me the folded sheet.

"I put an asterisk next to those who've spent the

night in my home. They're the only ones who could've known what I eat every morning. Also, I think the person must've taken a key to my house and made a copy. I leave the house locked, and there was no sign of forced entry. Yesterday I had all the locks changed, just in case."

I didn't tell her that with a little skill and the right picks, a person could break into most homes with relative ease without leaving a trace. I unfolded the single sheet and my eyes widened. It seemed Allison Crane was sleeping with, or had slept with, over half of her current staff. Of the seven names on the list, five had asterisks.

"Well, gee. This narrows it down." I tried not to grin.

"I was afraid you'd say something like that." This time, the blush was unmistakable. "Keep in mind that's over a long period of time. I mean, it's not like I was sleeping with them all at the same time."

"Any of them still pining away?" I asked. "Any feel jilted? Jealous perhaps?"

"I really don't think so. Like I said, I've been honest about how much I can give. I don't think anyone harbors ill feelings toward me."

Except that obviously somebody did. "When exactly does this retreat take place?" I asked.

Her voice was suddenly girlish. "Tomorrow."

"Tomorrow?" I was incredulous. Could I possibly get everything together in time?

But Allison was beaming. "Then you'll do it? Oh, thank you! I was afraid you were going to say no. I've already arranged for your cabin. There was a last-minute cancellation, and with a little maneuvering, I managed to get us an adjoining suite. That way, you can keep an eye on my room." She was positively radiant.

"Looks like you've thought of everything," I said, slightly miffed. I wasn't used to other people making my decisions.

Allison seemed to sense my mood. "I can't tell you how grateful I am." She got up and came to stand in front of me. "I know you're not eager to take this case, but you really are my best chance. Even if you're not able to figure out who's trying to kill me, you can at least act as my bodyguard. Just knowing you'll be there, I feel a hundred percent better. In fact, I think I'm even starting to look forward to the retreat again. It really is one of the prettiest places I've ever been. You'll like it."

Her whole countenance had changed and her face lit up with enthusiasm. It was hard to resist her. I got directions and instructions about what to bring on the trip. I went over my fees with her and she wrote me a ridiculously large check as a retainer.

"In case the murderer is successful," she said, "and I'm unable to pay you the rest."

"If she is, then I won't have done my job," I said, sounding more confident than I felt.

"But at least you're willing to try. That's all I can ask."

I walked her out to her boat and we stood on the dock facing each other. Ospreys dove for fish in the sunlit water, making giant splashes, while others circled overhead filling the air with their cries. Allison's eyes seemed to sparkle in the sun and for the second time that morning, we shook hands.

"Thank you, Ms. James," she said.

"You might as well call me Cassidy," I said, "seeing as how we're going to become sweethearts." I grinned and untied the rope, tossing it in the little boat. I shoved her off and watched the boat slice across the water until it was out of view. Then I marched back up to the house, planning my verbal assault on Martha.

Chapter Three

"It was not my idea!" Martha insisted. "I told her to call the police in Portland. Even gave her a name. She said she needed someone she could trust, someone who could maybe go undercover. It was her idea, Cass. I just gave her your name. Honest."

It was impossible for me to stay mad at Martha. I sighed.

"How'd you get out of it?" she asked.

"I didn't."

"You mean you're going? Really?"

"You think I shouldn't?" I was already regretting my decision.

"Actually, I think there's a chance it'll work. If someone really is trying to kill her, she could use some protection. And posing as her girlfriend will allow you to blend into the woodwork. I'd volunteer myself, except too many people know I'm a cop. Too bad you can't take Maggie, though. I hear that retreat is really something."

"How come you're not going?" Martha rarely missed an event sponsored by Women On Top.

"The place is booked like a decade in advance. I'm surprised she was able to get you a cabin."

"Well, she is the president. I think she pulled some strings."

"Come to think of it, there's not much that Allison Crane couldn't pull off, once she set her mind to it. She's a special lady, Cass. It's hard to imagine anyone wanting to hurt her, let alone kill her. But after talking to her, I don't think she's imagining these attacks. You want me to take care of the beasts?"

"No, I'll get Rick and Towne to do it. They're closer. Besides, Rick likes to take them out to their house. Towne's even thinking of getting him a kitten for his birthday. This would be a good trial session."

"Have you told Maggie yet?" Martha asked.

"Not yet. I was anxious to yell at you," I said. "Oh, damn."

"What?"

"I just remembered. Our anniversary is next weekend."

"I'm sure Maggie will understand, Cass. This is,

after all, a pretty important case. You can celebrate when you get back."

"I know. But after all the hassles we went through to start with, this anniversary is kind of special."

"Of all the women in the world, Cass, Maggie Carradine will understand. She's a shrink, for God's sake. They can handle life's little disappointments."

Buoyed by that remark, I called Maggie as soon as I hung up from Martha.

"A whole week?" Her disappointment knifed through me.

"It's a life-and-death kind of thing. Someone is trying to kill the poor woman."

"What kind of retreat is this?"

"Uh, it's like a corporate retreat, I guess. Different organizations rent it out."

"And which organization does this client belong to?" She was trying to be polite, but her voice had an edge.

"Women On Top," I muttered.

"What?" I could just imagine her green eyes flashing. "You're going on a lesbian retreat? For a week? Were you going to skip that part?"

"Of course not," I said, not sure if it was true. "I just hadn't gotten to it yet. Don't get weird on me, Mag, this is just a job."

She heaved a heavy sigh. "I know, Cass. I can't help it, though. It's my one little character flaw. If not for being jealous, I'd be perfect."

"This is true. In fact, even with your one little character flaw, you are perfect. I promise, I won't even look at any of the women there. My job is to figure out who's trying to kill this woman, and as soon as I do, I'm out of there."

"What's she look like?"

"Who?"

"This poor little client. You make her sound old and frail. I just wondered what she looked like."

"Uh, well. She's got red hair and she's about my height. On the thin side. In her late thirties, I'd guess."

"Oh, terrific."

"What?"

"She's gorgeous, isn't she?"

"Not at all. Why would you think such a thing?"

"What is she, a secretary or something?"

"You mean for Women On Top? She's the president."

"The president. How nice. And what does she do for a living, pray tell?" Maggie's voice had taken on a distinctly caustic tone, and I wondered just how long the incident with Erica Trinidad was going to haunt both of us.

"She's an M.D.," I mumbled.

"Oh, lovely, a doctor. This is nice. A presidential doctor. A gorgeous red headed presidential M.D. Poor little thing. No wonder she needs big strong Cassidy James to protect her."

"Maggie, you're definitely getting weird here. The woman is being stalked by someone in her organization. Her job and title have nothing to do with it. Neither does her hair color. Would you feel better if she were a poor, ugly, bald trash collector?"

"Yes," she said. To my relief, she started to laugh and so did I. "I'll miss you, that's all," she said.

"I'll miss you, too. I guess we'll have to celebrate our anniversary when I get back."

"Our anniversary?"

"You didn't remember?" I was crushed.

"Of course I remembered, you bozo. You thought I'd forget something as significant as this? I may have a slight jealous streak, but I'm not a schmuck!"

I had a feeling I'd be spending a good part of the rest of my life battling that "slight jealous streak," and the thought warmed me. I could live with it. In fact, I was looking forward to it. I told her so, and she laughed.

By the time we hung up, I was pretty sure she knew that I loved her beyond reason. Thank God I hadn't mentioned the part about me posing as Allison's girlfriend. If she knew that, I might as well not even bother to come back.

Chapter Four

Monday came so quickly, I barely had enough time to get my things in order. Allison had told me to pack lightly, that the second leg of the journey was by horseback and that all of our belongings would be brought up the mountain by mule.

"What kind of resort is this?" I asked. I'd been picturing hordes of women lying by the pool on chaise lounges sipping piña coladas.

"Rustic," she'd answered, "but incredibly well-stocked. It's high up in the mountains and totally secluded which is part of the charm. Even having to ride the horses adds to the sense of being away from the real world. People pay a lot of money for the privilege of roughing it in style. It gets cold at night, though, so bring some warm clothes. Mount Hood is just over the hill."

So I'd thrown in jeans, sweats, a swim suit, two nice outfits, a jacket, and a couple of pairs of shoes. I didn't want to overload my bag with clothes, because I also wanted to take along some new surveillance gadgets I'd bought but hadn't had the occasion to use. Unfortunately, the extra equipment made my bag a little heavy.

"Jesus, what do you have in this thing?" Towne complained, hefting the bag over his shoulder. He worked out on Nautilus three times a week, so I didn't think he was in any trouble. Still, I worried about the mules.

"I've got a pair of binoculars that look like sunglasses," I said, pleased he'd asked. "And a really cool video cam that's so small I can hide it almost anywhere. Also, a pretty neat tape recorder that can transmit sounds within a thirty-foot radius back to wherever I happen to have my cordless phone. I just hope they have phone service up there. If not, my laptop won't be of much use. I guess it is kind of heavy."

"No gun?" he asked, mustache twitching with humor.

"Oh, well, yeah, that too. You sure you can manage?"

He rolled his eyes and swung around toward the living room. Rick was sitting in my favorite blue swivel chair, both cats huddled on his lap.

"We're really gonna miss you," he said.

"Yeah, I can tell. Come here. All three of you."

Rick obediently carried both cats over to where I stood while Towne carried my bag down to the boat. I rubbed Gammon between the ears and scratched Panic's chin. I stood on my toes and kissed Rick on the cheek.

"You painting anything yet?"

Ever since a madman had sliced up all of his paintings a year ago, Rick had been unable to start painting again. Towne had saved the shredded pictures, and was trying to get some of them repaired, unbeknownst to Rick. No one was pressuring him, but the longer he went on without picking up a paintbrush, the more everyone worried. Maggie, who'd been his therapist years ago, had started working with him again, though she'd been hesitant because of their friendship. Recently, she'd confided that she thought it was doing some good.

"I have some ideas," he said, "but I don't want to jinx them by talking about them. Who knows? Maybe by the time you get back, I'll have one done."

"Oh, Rick." I didn't dare say anything more. Maggie kept insisting that the worst thing we could do was to put pressure on him. So I squeezed his hand and turned away before he could see the emotion in my eyes.

"Don't worry about us, we'll be fine!" he called. I knew the cats would be. It was Rick I worried about.

"He says he has some ideas," I told Towne as I got into my Sea Swirl.

"He's been holed up in there for a week now. Won't let me in and won't talk about what he's doing. I just hope to God he's actually painting. But I'm scared, Cass. What if it's terrible? I mean, what if he's really lost it?"

Towne's eyes were sad even when he was happy. At the moment, they looked positively mournful.

"You can't lose your creative touch, I don't think. Besides, anything Rick Parker does is beautiful. Quit worrying, Towne. If he's holing himself up, it's definitely a good sign. Does Maggie know?"

"I'll call her tonight," he said.

"Well, tell her I miss her already, and that I looked like hell, I was so lonely. Okay?"

"Actually, I was thinking you looked pretty damned perky."

I reached down and splashed him with water.

"But I'll tell her you were death warmed over."

"Thanks, buddy. Take care." I eased the throttle into forward and pulled away from my dock, feeling like a kid leaving for summer camp, suddenly scared, lonely and regretting the whole thing.

But this was, I reminded myself, precisely why I'd let Martha talk me into becoming a P.I. in the first place. There was someone in danger and I might just be able to do something about it. A ridiculously noble thought, I knew, but the very hogwash that drove me.

So I stuffed my other emotions back where I could ignore them and pushed the throttle forward, letting the wind whip my face as I sped across the lake. I'd have enjoyed it more, but my mind suddenly returned to the dream and I couldn't shake the feeling that it was trying to warn me of something dreadful.

* * * * *

It was a nice day for a drive. There were a few fluffy clouds high in the sky, but the sun was strong and except for an occasional logging truck, traffic was light. The road followed the Umpqua River through thick stands of Douglas fir and cedar. Herds of giant-antlered elk grazed in protected clearings, and ospreys fished along the riverbank. I rolled the windows down and let the cool air rush in, singing along with a Sophie B. Hawkins CD, the volume cranked up.

When I reached Interstate Five, I drove north, pushing my Jeep Cherokee past the speed limit, keeping one eye on the mirror for cops. By the time I reached Portland, I was famished. All I'd had that morning was a piece of toast and some coffee. I looked at the map and did some quick calculations. I'd have to hurry to reach the base camp by three. If I didn't make it, I'd have to wait until morning and join the non-horse riders on a bus ride that Allison said took even longer than the horse trail because it wound half-way around the mountain. And I'd promised Allison I'd be there tonight. Ignoring the growling in my stomach as I passed a McDonalds, I pressed onward.

When at last I made the turnoff, I was surprised at how quickly civilization was left behind. The road became a two-lane strip of asphalt that twisted and climbed through towering trees. I was beginning to wonder if I'd ever get there, when suddenly the road flattened out and the trees gave way to a lush meadow. I drove over a cattle grate and under im-

29

pressive wooden arches that sported a giant T intersected by a bone. I had finally made it to the T-Bone Ranch, the base camp for the Eagle's Nest Resort. With about ten minutes to spare. Damn, I thought, I could have stopped for that hamburger.

I followed the driveway to a large dirt lot where at least fifty cars were already parked. Allison had told me that she'd be going up with the majority of the women in the morning shift. Three o'clock was the final run of the day, and the rest of the people would come up on Tuesday by bus. I locked the Jeep and hefted my bag over my shoulder, hoping they hadn't left without me.

"Looks like you just made it," a Stetsoned man called out, hurrying over. "Here, let me get that for you." I gladly handed him my bag and felt a little guilty when he grunted under the unexpected weight.

"They're already mounted up. Can you ride?" He eyeballed my cowboy boots and I was glad I'd worn them. They were scuffed and well-worn, proof that I wasn't just a "drugstore" cowgirl.

"A little." In truth I was a pretty decent rider.

"Good. 'Cause the only horse left is Diablo, and he's mean as spit. You look like you can handle him, though. This your first time here?"

He led me around the perimeter of a string of ranch-style buildings toward the stables. A hundred yards to the south, I saw the incongruous form of a helicopter resting on a round concrete pad.

"Somebody fly in?" I asked.

"Nah, that's for emergencies. In case someone gets sick at the resort. Takes too long to get 'em down, otherwise. The only road up beside the horse trail is an old dirt fire road and even in a four wheel drive, it takes several hours."

When we turned the corner, my guide started to chuckle. A short, middle-aged woman was attempting to climb onto a rather large palomino, and while she'd managed to get one foot in the stirrup, she couldn't quite pull herself up. Her lover stood behind her, pushing her rump in a vain attempt to assist, but the palomino wasn't helping.

"I better go give 'em a hand. Here. Take this over to Buddy, that boy with the black hat, and tell him to give you Diablo." He handed me my bag and I tried diligently not to grunt under the weight. Maybe I should have gone a little easier on the surveillance stuff, I thought, looking for the black hat.

I couldn't help but notice that most of the women were already saddled up and watching my every move. I wondered if they'd been told to arrive earlier than three. Some of them didn't look too happy to see me, like it was my fault they'd been kept waiting. I smiled winningly and tried to ignore the scowls.

"I'm supposed to ask for Diablo," I said, handing my bag to a skinny red-headed kid in a black cowboy hat.

"Nobody in their right mind asks for Diablo. But seeing as he's the only horse left, I guess he'll have to do. Anyone else comes, they'll have to ride a mule."

Despite my ease around horses, I was starting to get a little nervous. "What's the matter with Diablo?"

Buddy chuckled and led me to the only horse tied to the railing — a jet-black gelding with a beautiful black mane and tail. His coat glistened in the sun and he pawed the ground nervously as we approached. His eyes were wild, the whites rolling back as he followed my every move.

"Nice Diablo," I crooned, patting his neck. The horse snorted and pawed the ground again, just missing my toe.

"He don't like strangers," the kid said.

Oh, great. What was he doing transporting strangers to a resort then? I was beginning to wonder about this resort. So far, the customer services seemed a little lacking. "Does he buck?" I asked, taking the reins.

"If he does, just hang onto that horn there and try to ride it out. He mostly prefers to rear though. Same thing, hang onto the horn and lean forward. He's okay unless he gets nervous. If the rider stays calm, so does he. You're not nervous are you?"

"You're kidding, right?" I held the reins with my left hand, put my left toe in the stirrup and swung myself into the saddle. Diablo's ears went straight back. Before he could think about rearing up, I nudged him sharply with my heels and clicked my tongue. He lunged forward, responding beautifully to the command.

"All right!" The kid grinned. I pulled back on the reins, and Diablo came to an abrupt halt. I backed him up a good ten paces. I turned him sharply to the left, then a full circle to the right. I reached down and patted his neck, my heart pounding. I knew every woman there was watching me, and I was slightly chagrinned to be showing off so blatantly. "Guess you done proved me wrong," Buddy said, patting Diablo on the butt.

The sudden movement surprised the horse and without any warning, his hind legs kicked out, narrowly missing the kid's head. I tried to calm him, but he wasn't having any of it. His muscles bunched beneath the saddle and he bucked with all his might. I felt my body leaving the saddle and forced my legs to hold on. My head was inches above the black mane, my left hand grasping at it as my right hand flailed wildly for balance. I felt my rear slam back down on the saddle and just had time to dig in with my knees when he bucked again. This time I was more prepared for the jolt that rocked me. I was vaguely aware of other voices and the people around me, but every fiber of my being was honed in on the beast beneath me. When his rear went up, I went with it. When he twisted to the left, I let myself twist along with him. I made myself a part of him, an extension of his own craziness. When at last he came to a stop, my heart was thudding and every muscle in my body ached.

The sound of applause was spontaneous and brought me back to reality. I looked around at the grinning faces and acknowledged the whoops and hollers with a grin of my own.

"Anybody want to trade horses?" I asked. They responded with laughter.

"Sorry about that," Buddy said, inching around Diablo, leaving a wide berth. "I guess I kinda spooked him. You okay?"

I shot the kid a fierce look and gently nudged Diablo with my heels, easing him forward. The next time he kicked at the little turkey, I hoped he connected.

"That was quite a show. Talk about a grand entrance. What are you going to do for an encore?" The woman was tall and athletic with short black hair brushed straight back off her high forehead. She had dark skin with light gold eyes and a wide smile.

The big red mare she sat on looked as gentle as a plow horse. I eyed her horse with envy and stretched my back. "Well, if I can still walk, I hope to hobble to the nearest jacuzzi, provided they have one, and soak for about two hours."

She laughed. "Not only do they have one, they're all over the place. Natural hot springs. Smell like sulphur, but you get used to it. I take it this is your first time?"

"If the beginning is any indication of how the rest of the week is going to go, it no doubt will be my last, too." She laughed again, and we got in line with the others who were finally beginning to move forward in a long, slow procession up the trail.

"Karen Castillo," she said, leaning over her saddle. I shook the proffered hand, wondering where I'd heard that name before.

"Cassidy James," I said. "You've been here before?"

"This is my third time. It's quite a place, once we finally get there. It takes a good hour and a half on this trail. By then, we'll all be ready for a cold beer and a hot bath. Wait till you see the lake! And the waterfalls! Eagle's Nest is the best kept secret in Oregon."

Diablo, apparently tuckered out from his temper tantrum, was as docile as a cow, and I held the reins loosely, enjoying the peaceful pace and the scenery.

"So, what do you do for a living?" she asked. "Professional cowgirl?"

"Cute," I said. "Actually I'm in real estate." This popped out of my mouth before I could think it through. I hoped she didn't ask me any questions about escrow or mortgages. "How about you?"

"I'm a teacher," she said. "And track coach."

"High school?" I asked. She nodded. Now that I thought about it, she did look kind of like a P.E. teacher. I wondered how many little jocks fell in love with her each year. I remembered my own track coach fondly and smiled. Suddenly I remembered where I had heard her name. I hadn't actually heard it. I'd seen it. On Allison's list. Karen Castillo was one of the officers for Women On Top, one with an asterisk next to her name, I thought, smiling. "So, how did you first hear about this resort?" I asked. The path had grown quite steep, and we were forced to proceed single file. I let her go in front.

"Women On Top comes up here every year," she said over her shoulder. "For the staff, it's sort of a working vacation. We plan the next year's events, attend some workshops, but mostly we relax and enjoy."

"You work with Women On Top?" I hoped I sounded only mildly interested.

"I'm the public relations officer. Fancy title, but mostly all I do is make up brochures and flyers and write ads for newspapers across the state. Don't tell anyone, but I use the school's Xerox machine to make copies. If they only knew!" She looked back, gold eyes crinkling with mischief.

"Sounds exciting," I said. "I mean, working with Women On Top. How'd you get involved with them?"

"I was recruited. A friend of mine, Reeva Dunsmoore, talked me into helping out on a lecture they were organizing about three years ago. 'Just this once,' she said. Ha! Three years later, here I am, still making flyers and writing ads. But I'm not complaining. It's a good group to work with."

The trail had become treacherous, with hairpin turns every hundred feet or so. On our left was a solid granite wall looming skyward. On our right, a three-hundred-foot drop. I'd have felt a lot better on Karen's red mare than on the black monster beneath me. One little buck on this stretch of ground and it would be a quick trip to the bottom.

No one was doing much talking now that the trail had narrowed, which gave me a chance to think. Reeva Dunsmoore was the vice president that Allison said had the greatest motive to want her out of the picture . . . and one of the few Allison hadn't slept with over the years. If Reeva had recruited Karen into the group, perhaps she'd had more than a professional interest in her. Karen had been one of Allison's lovers, so it was possible that there was a jealousy factor involved. Maybe Reeva wasn't just irked about Allison's politics, maybe she was hurting over the loss of Karen's love.

I continued on in this vein, making up wild scenarios in which Reeva, or one of the other women I'd yet to meet, plotted Allison Crane's death. The thing I kept coming back to, though, was why? What was the motive? Who would benefit from Allison's death? Which made me wonder about money. Allison said she didn't have any family. If that were true, then who would be the beneficiary of her estate? Doctors made pretty decent wages, and I imagined there'd be some life insurance too. I put that on my mental list of things to ask Allison, if and when we ever got to the damned resort. My stomach had given up growling. It had started to whimper.

When we finally arrived, I forgot my hunger and even my aching muscles as I gazed at the beauty around me. Karen hadn't lied. Eagle's Nest Resort was spectacular.

On the north side of the valley, a pristine emerald lake glistened in the afternoon sun. In the middle of the lake was a tiny island, thick with cedar and fir. Running right through the valley was a good-sized stream, flat boulders strewn like stepping stones peeking out of the water. The roar of a distant waterfall could be heard above the rustling pines. In the distance, Mount Hood, huge and majestic, towered over the valley like a benevolent giant.

To our right was the resort itself. The main building was a large pine lodge with an expansive deck facing the lake. Smoke curled out of the rock chimney and the aroma of a barbecue somewhere nearly made me weep with happiness. Women lounged on porch swings and strolled the grounds, quite a few of them coming over to greet the new arrivals.

Surrounding the lodge on all sides, all the way down to the lake, were dozens of tiny cabins nestled among the trees. The paths leading to each cabin were bordered by geraniums and pansies, and whenever one of the paths crossed the stream, a wooden footbridge arched across it.

Every so often I thought I caught the faint but distinctive odor of sulphur floating on the breeze. Sure enough, interspersed among the trees, tell-tale puffs of steam rose from the hot tubs behind the cabins. If this wasn't paradise, it was close to it. I eased myself out of the saddle and patted Diablo's sweaty neck. The horse eyed me suspiciously for a moment, then arched his neck toward me, showing me where to scratch.

"You're nothing but a big baby," I teased, scratching behind his ears. He showed me his teeth and nickered softly.

"I think he likes you," a woman said, startling me. "Kind of a love-hate relationship, huh?" I turned to see a plain-looking woman grinning down at me from her horse. Her mousy brown hair was streaked with gray and tied back in a ponytail that hung nearly to the saddle. Her gray eyes held amusement.

"Uh, this is Fay Daniels," Karen said. "She's our newest staff member, which means she's stuck with all the grunt work. This is Cassidy James, cowgirl extraordinaire."

"Glad to meet you," Fay said, reaching down to extend a calloused hand. Her fingers were thick and sturdy. I thought of Allison's list, trying to recall if there'd been an asterisk next to Fay's name. I didn't think so. Maybe because she was new to the group, I thought.

Karen climbed off her big red mare and stretched her legs. I hadn't realized just how tall she was until Fay dismounted and stood next to her. Karen was lanky next to Fay's sturdy, squarish frame.

"If I don't eat soon, I'm going to faint," I admitted. "How do meals work around here?"

"Two ways," Karen said. "First, every cabin has a little fridge that's kept fairly well-stocked and a kitchenette. Also, there's a mini-mart inside the lodge, so you can re-stock the basics. Then there's the dining room which serves breakfast, lunch and dinner. Dinner's not until seven, though, so if you're really starving, you'd better grab something from the mini-mart or see what's in your fridge. Didn't you read all this in the brochure?"

I thought quickly. "Actually, I never saw the brochure. A couple of friends chipped in and treated me as a surprise. I just found out about it a few days ago."

"Must be pretty good friends. This place isn't cheap," Fay said. "If officers didn't get half-price, I'm not sure I could afford it."

"At least we can write it off as a business expense," Karen said. "Allison keeps reminding us not to call it a vacation, but a working retreat."

The ranch hands who had been leading the horses into a large corral finally came and took ours away. I started to pat Diablo on the rear but thought better of it. No sense pushing my luck.

"Which cabin is yours?" Karen asked.

"Something called Cascade. Any idea which direction I should go?"

"No clue. But you can ask in the lodge. You could wander around for days before you'd find it. I'm in Mother Goose, which is off to the right, I think. Maybe we'll see you at dinner?"

"If I haven't passed out from hunger, I'll be there."

I watched them walk away, Karen's long legs taking sure strides toward her cabin, her suitcase balanced on her shoulder, with Fay working to keep pace beside her. Neither looked like a killer, I thought. But then again, Jeffrey Dahmer hadn't looked like a cannibal either. I knew from past experiences that first impressions weren't always all they were cracked up to be.

Chapter Five

The woman at the registration desk was wearing a red-checkered flannel shirt with pearl snap buttons and a pair of well-worn jeans tucked into boots. She had turquoise rings on nearly every finger, a turquoise bracelet on each wrist and even a turquoise bolo around her neck. Her black hair was shot through with gray and tied back with a red scarf. Her face was as weather-beaten as a rancher's. She gave me directions to Cascade, which she assured me was one of the nicer cabins. "Not that they're not all nice," she added hastily in a raspy, smoker's voice.

"Don't I need a key?"

"The room's unlocked, but there's a key on the table. A lot of people like to get right to their cabin after riding up here. If we made everyone check in first, it would just make their wait that much longer."

"Someone said there was a mini-mart where I could buy something to eat?"

"Oh, honey, you don't need to shop yet. Just check your icebox."

It had been years since I'd heard anyone refer to a refrigerator as an ice box. I smiled and went in search of my cabin.

She was right. Cascade sat high on a knoll, in a small clearing surrounded by trees. The afternoon sun was beating down on the porch and the stream ran right in front of it. I stood for a minute enjoying the view, not just of the nature around me, but of the many women meandering by. With a sudden pang, I wished with all my heart that Maggie had come with me.

I turned back toward the cabin, a rustic pine and cedar duplex. Allison said she'd gotten us a suite, but this was really two separate cabins with a common wall. The shared porch was divided by a rock retainer so people in both cabins could sit out front and maintain their privacy.

When I pushed open the door, I was pleasantly surprised. I'd expected rugged furnishings, but the place was quite homey. I stepped into what was essentially one large room and noticed logs already laid in the fireplace. The bay windows looked out to the lake and let sunlight into the room. There was a tiny but serviceable kitchen in the far corner and a queen-sized bed against the other wall. But a quick survey told me what I'd feared. There was no phone in the room. It seemed I'd hauled my fancy tape recording equipment and laptop up here for nothing. So much for long-range sleuthing. I'd have to rely on gathering information from the women themselves. Without going one step farther, I set my bag on the floor and headed straight for the fridge. I practically fainted with happiness. It was loaded!

I twisted off the cap of a Miller High Life and took a deep swallow. Then, telling myself to calm down, I began creating. I started with sardines on cream-cheese-covered Ritz crackers. Delicious. I added sun-dried tomatoes dripping with olive oil to a few crackers and ate them as I stood, still looking in the fridge. I found a ripe red apple and was about to bite into it when there was a sudden noise behind me. I turned to see Allison Crane staring at me, laughing.

"Don't you knock?" I said, feeling my face redden. I wondered how long she'd been standing there watching me gorge myself.

"Sorry. I thought I heard you come in. I was out back, taking a soak." Indeed, she was wrapped loosely in a green terry robe and her red curls were damp at the edges.

"Out back?"

She walked over and helped herself to a sardine and cracker. "In the hot tub. It's very private. One of the reasons I wanted this particular cabin. That and the fact that it's a suite."

Now that I was no longer in danger of keeling over, I looked around and noticed that she'd come into my room through the bathroom. There were two doors to the bathroom, one on my side, the other on hers.

"We share a bathroom?" I asked, finally biting into the apple.

"Yes, but you can lock your door from your side. In case you're afraid I might steal something." She grinned, hugging her robe around her.

I walked through to Allison's cabin, a mirror image of my own, except hers already looked well-lived in. In fact, there was hardly a surface that wasn't covered with some article of clothing. A bra dangled over the back of the chair in front of the fireplace. A pair of panties had been tossed on the bed. Several shirts adorned the little kitchen table and a pair of jeans lay on the floor. When I arched an eyebrow, she giggled.

"I was having trouble deciding what to wear," she said.

I looked at her robe and grinned. "Good choice."

"I mean for dinner tonight." She tightened the belt on her robe a bit self-consciously and straightened her hair. "I brought some pictures for you to look at before dinner. So you'll know who's who. I thought you could kind of check everyone out during dinner, size them up."

"Allison, please. Let me decide what I'm going to do, okay?"

She looked up, hurt. "Oh. Well, sure. I mean, of course. I didn't mean to tell you how to do your job."

"It's okay," I said, feeling guilty. "Actually, that's

exactly what I had in mind anyway. By the way, I noticed there's no phone in the room. Do you know where the closest one is?"

"Back down the mountain at the T-Bone Ranch. There's a two-way radio in the lodge they use to contact the ranch but even cell phones don't work up here. It's part of the allure of the resort. All these business women and no phones! They don't know what to do with themselves the first few days. Half of them cart their laptops all the way up here, even though the brochure is very explicit about the facilities." I decided not to mention my own laptop. It wasn't really my fault. I hadn't seen the brochure.

"A lot of people just can't imagine a place this isolated," she went on. "For me, the isolation and privacy are what make it so special. People really connect up here. Don't worry, Stella can radio down if you need something." While she talked, she held the top of her robe together in her fist and it suddenly dawned on me that she was probably naked beneath it.

"Let me know when you want to look at those pictures," I said, turning back to my room.

"How about now?"

"Maybe you should get dressed first," I suggested. Her cheeks colored.

"And I want to get myself unpacked anyway. Give me thirty minutes, okay?"

"Take your time. I'm going back out to the hot tub."

I hadn't meant to hurt her feelings, but I definitely didn't want to give her the wrong idea. Posing as her girlfriend was going to be hard enough. The last thing we needed was to complicate matters by letting real feelings surface. I thought again of Maggie, suddenly missing her as if I'd been gone a week already.

It didn't take long to put my stuff away. As I hung up my clothes, I saw that my closet also backed up to Allison's. By standing in the closet and peering out through the slats, I could see into my room. If I were to make a small hole in the closet wall, I was pretty sure I'd be able to look from my closet into Allison's, and through the slatted door of her closet into her room. If I were to tape my video cam to the hole, I should have a pretty clear shot of her cabin from my closet, as long as none of her clothes were in the way.

I went out to the kitchen and rummaged around until I found a good, sturdy knife. Outside, I found a suitable rock. I carried these to the closet, selected an eye-level site, and began hammering at the wall inside the closet. I was glad Allison had opted to go back outside. I hadn't decided yet whether or not I wanted her to know about the camera.

The hole turned out to be a little bigger than I'd intended, but I didn't think it would be too obvious. I used the duct tape I'd brought to hold the camera in place against the closet wall. I'd also thought to bring an extension cord, but plugging it in would mean that whoever came into my room would see the cord and wonder why I needed it in the closet. The battery was good for a few hours, but would need constant recharging. I decided I'd just have to play it by ear, plugging it in whenever I could, tossing the cord in the closet whenever someone entered. It shouldn't be too much trouble, though. The camera was equipped with an electronic motion sensor and only started taping when the sensor picked up movement in the room.

The other problem was Allison's clothes. I'd lined up the camera so that the wide-angle lens had a clear view between the slats, but what if she moved her clothes? Of course, given the fact she seemed to prefer them strewn around the room, this might not be a problem.

For now, without moving the camera at all, I could see almost the entire cabin, with the exception of one corner of the kitchen. I was still fooling around with the focus when Allison came back in. Her hair was damp and the curls were stuck to her forehead. Her skin was pink from the heat of the tub, and perspiration dotted her brow. Suddenly, I realized I was spying on her and hurried to turn the camera off, feeling like a peeping Tom. But not before I'd seen the robe drop, and Allison's heat-flushed body beneath.

A half-hour later, when she knocked on our adjoining door, she was dressed smartly in well-fitting slacks and a navy blazer. I had showered and changed from my riding clothes into a pair of white twill pants, white shirt with sleeves rolled up to my elbows, and a tan vest. Martha called this my off-to-the-races look. Maggie said it showed off my tan. I called it wrinkle-free wash-and-wear.

"Ready?" she said, letting her gaze slide over me. I willed myself not to blush, ignoring the bold appraisal, and led her to the tiny kitchen table where we spent more than an hour poring over her pictures while I pumped her for information about her colleagues. By the time we were finished, I knew as much about most of the women as I knew about some of my own friends. But I was no closer to knowing which one of them might be trying to kill Allison.

Chapter Six

The dining room was already packed and the women kept pouring in. Allison had said they'd be sitting close to the stage at the far end because she was supposed to deliver a brief welcome speech. The plan was for me to find a spot close enough to her table that I could study the women in her group. After dinner, I was supposed to come over and ask her to dance, thus beginning our charade.

I was still standing in the main entry, trying to find her table, when somebody clapped me on the back. I turned and smiled at Karen Castillo, dressed in a black turtleneck and black jeans. With her black hair brushed back off her forehead, she looked like a female Johnny Cash. I immediately recognized the woman with her as Reeva Dunsmore, the mechanic and vice president of Women On Top.

"Hey, cowgirl. You find your cabin okay? This is the one I told you about," she said, winking at Reeva. "Chastity, right?"

"Cassidy," I corrected. "Cassidy James."

"Reeva Dunsmore," Reeva said. She didn't offer a hand, but rather tossed her chin back in greeting. Her yellow hair was shaved into a flattop, and her right ear was graced with half a dozen diamond studs. She wore an unbuttoned flannel shirt over a white ribbed muscle shirt tucked into Levis which were tucked into ankle-high hiking boots. Her mouth was smallish, adding to the rather rough look she projected. "I hear you put on quite a show this afternoon," she said, but her gray eyes had already dismissed me, and even as she spoke, she was scanning the crowd.

"Come sit at our table," Karen offered. "When you're up here by yourself, it's easier if you've got someone to introduce you around." She put her arm around my shoulder and steered me through the milling crowd. So much for plans, I thought, inwardly smiling at this turn of events. Now I'd be able to do more than just keep an eye on things.

When Allison saw me walk up with Karen and Reeva, she raised an eyebrow and then turned back toward Billie Slater, who was engaged in an animated story as we took our seats. I recognized Billie from the photographs. A light-skinned African-American with close-cropped hair and long dangly earrings, she had intelligent, walnut-colored eyes and an easy smile. She wore all white and had a handful of bracelets on her wrist that jangled when she gestured. Allison had said she was a professional photographer, but my first glance told me she was on the wrong end of the camera.

"So I said, 'You know why straight women are so bad at math? Because for years they've been told that this is ten inches.'" She held her thumb and forefinger an inch apart and everyone at the table laughed. "I'm Billie Slater," she said, turning her smile toward me. "Which one of these lucky bums just snagged you?"

It was my turn to laugh. "I'm Cassidy James. And thanks for the compliment. Actually, Karen was nice enough to invite me to share your table. We rode up the trail together today. I'm afraid I don't know a soul here."

"Well, you do now. This is Allison Crane, the president of our little organization. And this is Lacy Watkins, our chief office assistant."

"Glorified secretary is more like it," Lacy said, gracing me with a slightly buck-toothed grin. I recognized her too. She was a short, curly-haired brunette with hazel eyes and a big, crescent-shaped dimple in each cheek. Allison had said she worked in the insurance industry as an independent adjustor. To me, she looked more like a tap dance instructor.

Allison stood and leaned across the table, offering her hand. I stood too.

"Any friend of Karen's," she said, squeezing my hand. Our eyes were locked and I was aware that others were watching us closely. I felt heat traveling up my neck.

"Thank you, it's a pleasure to meet you all," I said, trying to take my hand back.

"The pleasure's all ours," Allison said, finally letting me go. I nearly toppled backwards and I could feel the barely suppressed grins around me.

"Uh oh," someone muttered. I wasn't sure, but I thought it might have been Reeva.

Karen began telling about my Diablo incident, and I watched Allison listen attentively.

"So you're a real cowgirl?" Allison asked.

"Yeah," Reeva interjected. "She likes to ride wild things. The wilder the better." There was strained laughter, and I felt I was missing the joke.

Allison blushed. "I guess it's time to get started," she said, pushing away from the table. She made her way to the stage and took the microphone. I was relieved to have the attention off me and took the opportunity to look around the room. More than half of the expected hundred were already in attendance. I knew others would be coming up by bus tomorrow, and it was hard to imagine the place with so many women packed into it. As it was, the room was alive with laughter.

"May I have your attention, please," Allison said softly into the microphone. The room fell silent. "Thank you. I'm Allison Crane." The crowd burst into spontaneous applause, with a good deal of whistling and table pounding. When the noise died down, she continued. "President of Women On Top." She smiled and shook her head at the fresh wave of applause. I could see a blush creeping up her neck, whether from pleasure or modesty I couldn't tell. When they'd finally quieted, she went on.

"Some people say that Women On Top is committed to making sure all lesbians have access to success in the business world. That's not entirely true. We're not just committed to this cause. We're driven.

"Each and every one of us in this room knows what it was like as a kid to sit in a classroom devoid of role models, to read history books that never mentioned the contributions of a single lesbian, to watch the media stereotype us as laughable, homely spinsters.

"And while we sat in those classrooms, scared to death that someone would guess our terrible secret, there were more than likely at least two other students in the room feeling the same way. Even at the modest estimate of ten percent, in a class of thirty, there were probably two or three of us. We may not have always recognized each other then, but we've found each other now, and we can't afford to lose sight of each other ever again." Once again, the room filled with applause, but Allison held up her hands.

"This week is about reaching out. The women in this room represent different races and cultures, different careers and different talents. But what we share is the common desire to make our place in the world, and to make room for others like us until the day comes when no child will have to sit in a classroom wondering who her role models are."

This time the room exploded in applause and Allison bowed her head until the noise subsided. "As you attend the workshops this week, and participate in the team-building activities, think of the women we've yet to reach, who still feel isolated, unaware of our growing community. When we leave a week from now, it is my hope that each of us will take a renewed determination back with us. The determination to reach those women and make the world a better place for all of us." She held up her hands, silencing them one last time. "Oh, and one other thing. The staff here this week is one hundred percent lesbian-friendly, so be yourselves and enjoy the beauty around you, and no, I'm not just talking about the scenery." There were scattered chuckles before she added a final note. "Let's all make this a week to remember."

The whole room applauded and I joined in, feeling strangely moved.

"Nice job," Billie said, standing up to kiss Allison's cheek when she returned to our table.

"Absolutely brilliant," Lacy said. Her dimples were huge as she beamed at Allison.

Allison's cheeks were slightly flushed and her eyes danced with excitement. "Now that that's over, I think I'll have a glass of wine. Sabrina, would you do the honors?"

Sabrina Pepper was a slender, waifish type with long blond hair and timid blue eyes. She was another of Allison's past amours, and during the speech she had watched Allison's every move. She was sitting at the far end of the table where a bottle of Kendall-Jackson Chardonnay sat chilling in a silver bucket. At Allison's request, she passed the bottle, after filling her own glass.

"That's true what you said about kids in school not having role models," Karen said. "It makes me feel guilty for not coming out to my classes. But the parents would freak. And half the kids would be afraid I was looking at them in the shower. It's not worth it." She ran her fingers through her jet black hair and sat forward in her chair, propping her elbows on the table.

"I liked what you said about reaching out to those women who are still isolated," Billie added. "Sometimes we forget that not all of us have support groups."

Reeva cut in. "I still say ten percent is way too low. Half the dykes I know are married and don't even know they're queer. Nobody's even counting them, for God's sake."

"What? You're not saying Goddess anymore?" Holly McIntyre asked, joining us. A devilish grin played across her tanned face. She had wide-set, brown eyes that twinkled with intelligence, and her blond hair was cut in a style reminiscent of Farrah Fawcett. She was wearing an expensive tan blazer and matching slacks. From talking with Allison, I knew she was a journalist by trade and the director of finance for Women On Top.

Reeva scowled at her, and took a healthy swig of her beer.

"What did you think?" Billie asked, her dark eyes sparkling at me.

"Very impressive," I said truthfully, looking at Allison. "You seem to be genuinely respected by the women here. Maybe you should run for public office."

Allison threw back her head and laughed. "If the world were full of lesbians, I'd think about it."

"If the world were full of lesbians, you wouldn't have time," Holly said. This brought on another round of laughter, and though it was directed at her, Allison laughed right along with them.

"Pour yourself a glass of wine, Fay. It may be a working vacation, but no one's working tonight,"

Allison said. Fay Daniels still wore her hair in the long ponytail that nearly reached her buttocks, but I noticed she'd taken the time to braid it. She'd come in late, halfway through Allison's speech and looked embarrassed to have missed it. She poured herself a dollop of the wine and passed the bottle back, smiling shyly. Allison had said her new assistant was hard-working and bright, but she seemed out of place in this crowd, I thought. She was the only reserved one in the bunch.

Despite my earlier snack, I was still ravenous and was glad to see the food finally served. A waiter had come earlier to take our orders, the choices being limited but appealing. I'd opted for the lasagne and garlic bread with a glass of Cabernet Sauvignon, promising myself I'd drink just one glass, lest some-one try to off Allison at the table.

Through dinner, the conversation moved easily, and it didn't take me long to see a pattern in their behavior toward one another. Interestingly, they all seemed to be showing off for my benefit. It was clear that there were two camps: those who adored Allison, and those who seemed to envy or resent her. Reeva and Karen were the most obvious in their resent-ment, while Billie, Lacy and Sabrina seemed to be ardent supporters. Holly McIntyre, or Farrah, as I now thought of her, seemed to vacillate between admira- tion and biting sarcasm. And who could tell about Fay Daniels? She seldom spoke. The woman had an amazing capacity for listening. She'd shown me a glimpse of humor earlier, but since joining the group for dinner, she'd remained practically silent.

Almost before we'd finished eating, women at other tables had started to dance. The lights were dimmed and the music changed from classical to soft rock. Reeva pushed herself away from the table and strode purposely toward an Asian woman she'd been eyeing during dinner. They made an interesting couple, I thought. Reeva's yellow flat top bobbing a foot above the slender, darker woman's silky crown.

Karen watched her friend on the dance floor, then cleared her throat, slicked back her hair again and asked Sabrina to dance. Sabrina was clearly startled by the question. Then she smiled shyly, blew her bangs away from her forehead, and they joined the growing throng on the dance floor.

Allison kicked me under the table, and I nearly choked on my wine.

"Would you like to dance?" I managed, glaring at her.

She seemed to consider it for a moment, smiled and pushed back her chair. "I thought you'd never ask."

I was aware of others watching us, and not just the women at our table. It hadn't occurred to me, when I'd accepted the challenge of posing as Allison's new girlfriend, that I'd be the center of so much attention. I led her to the dance floor and held out my arms.

"You kick me under the table again, and I'm going to kick you back," I murmured, holding her somewhat tentatively. It was a medium-slow song, and while some women were attempting to fast-dance, most were dancing cheek-to-cheek.

"I thought you were going to sit there forever and I knew someone else would ask me to dance. I didn't mean to kick you so hard, however. Did I hurt you?" Rather than answer, I pulled her closer and turned her in a quick circle, liking the way she moved so easily. "For a cowgirl, you dance pretty well," she said into my ear. "Even if you do insist on leading."

"For a presidential doctor with about three million women in love with her, you follow okay." Her laugh was husky, contagious. "For what it's worth," I continued, "I don't think either Reeva or Karen is too fond of you. I thought you said none of your exes held grudges."

"Shhh. Let's just dance for now. You're supposed to act like you're enjoying this. Kiss my neck."

"What?"

"My neck. Or just nuzzle it. People are watching."

I twirled her again, then leaned toward her ear, whispering, "I don't nuzzle on command."

She giggled, and to my complete surprise, leaned closer and grazed my neck with her teeth. It wasn't so much her doing it that shocked me, but the way my damn body responded. Furious at myself, I decided to set her straight right then and there.

"Do that again and I'm out of here. I mean it." My voice surprised me. It cracked like an adolescent boy's.

"God, I'm sorry," she whispered. She sounded genuinely crushed.

I glared at her. "Just don't do that again." The song ended and I started to walk back, but Allison grabbed my hand and I had no choice but to dance with her. To my relief, it was a fast song. Even so, I had trouble getting into it.

Allison was having the time of her life, to all appearances, and in fact she was such a good dancer, it was hard to stay mad for long. The truth was, I loved to dance, and they were playing a song I particularly liked.

We were dancing fast, but our bodies were almost touching, and Allison was holding my hips with her hands, mirroring my moves. I tried valiantly to remember that this was role-playing and started to think I'd missed my calling. I certainly had people around us fooled. Even Karen, who was still dancing with Sabrina, flashed me the thumbs-up sign.

When the song ended, Allison leaned forward and kissed me on the lips. It was the world's quickest kiss, but not very many people missed it. As for me, I was mortified at the way my stomach flipped over.

"Let's get some air," I muttered, furious. Obviously, some rules needed to be set.

"Good idea." She held onto my hand and led me through the crowd, stopping to chat with what seemed like half the people in the room. By the time we got outside, I was somewhat calmed down. It had taken us forever.

"I think that went very well," she said. "You did all right, considering you were such an unwilling accomplice."

"Allison, listen," I said. We were walking toward the lake, away from the other women getting fresh air. "I am very happily involved with a wonderful woman. I have no intention or desire to be unfaithful. I think it's important we keep this on a professional level. Even if I weren't involved, I don't mess around with clients." Which was a big lie. Erica Trinidad had been my first client, and we'd done plenty of messing around.

She was so quiet I was afraid I'd hurt her

feelings. Finally, half-way to the lake, she turned to face me, her eyes fierce in the moonlight. "I just want you to catch whoever's trying to kill me, Cass. The sooner you do, the sooner we can quit pretending, and then maybe I can actually start enjoying myself."

"Look, I'm sorry. I just didn't want to give you the wrong idea. I mean, as long as you know where I'm coming from."

"No, you look. You're cute, but you're not that cute. Some people think I could have almost any woman I wanted. What on earth makes you think I'm suddenly crushed that you, of all people, aren't interested?"

"I never said I thought you were crushed. I just wanted to be upfront with you. I don't mind pretending. I just wanted to make sure you knew that's what I was doing."

"Trust me, Cassidy James. That's all I'm doing too. If and when I ever decide to quit pretending and act on how I really feel, you'll know the difference."

With that, she turned on her heel and headed back toward her cabin, and like a faithful watch-dog, I followed after her, my ears ringing with her words the whole way back.

Chapter Seven

I left Allison standing on her front porch staring
moodily out at the lake. All I wanted was a long
soak in the hot tub and a good night's sleep, but
first I wanted to check my video cam to see if she'd
had any visitors. I tossed my clothes onto the bed,
grabbed a robe from the hook by the bathroom and
stepped into the closet. Before I could even get my
eye to the lens, I heard Allison's front door open.
This was followed by a sudden shriek and a thud. I
raced through the adjoining bathroom in time to see
Allison slump to the floor. An unopened bottle of

wine lay on the floor next to her head, and she was moaning. The window was wide open, the curtains flapping in the breeze.

"Are you all right?" I asked. She nodded and moaned again, rubbing her shoulder. She didn't seem to be too badly hurt. I rushed to the window and looked out into the darkness.

"I'll be right back," I said, making up my mind. I belted my robe and dashed out the door. To the east, I saw a shadowy figure disappear into the woods. There was nothing but heavily wooded walking trails in that direction. Sending a quick prayer skyward, I ran after the retreating figure.

It didn't take me long to realize, however, that I was at a distinct disadvantage. For one thing, I wasn't wearing any shoes and the ground was covered with rocks, pine needles and pine cones. I also hadn't brought anything with me, such as a flashlight or the thirty-eight stashed in my closet. Nor did I have the vaguest idea where I was going. I stopped, listening to the sounds of the night, staring into the darkness. Then, using better judgment, I turned back.

Allison was sitting on one of the kitchen chairs. In her lap she held the bottle of wine that someone had obviously hit her with. On the table next to her was a small platter of pâte.

"Did you see who it was?" she asked.

I shook my head. "Too dark. By the time I got outside, they were already in the woods. Are you okay?"

"I dodged at the last second. As soon as I closed the door behind me, I sensed something and moved just fast enough to avoid having my skull crushed.

I've got a fairly deep contusion on my shoulder, though." She pulled back her blouse and showed me a rapidly swelling lump already turning blue. "If that bottle had connected with my head, I don't think either one would be in one piece. She had a vicious swing." She smiled, but her blue-green eyes looked frightened.

"Did you see her at all?"

She shook her head. "I walked in, turned to find the light switch on the wall and got hit from behind. It took the breath right out of me. By the time I knew what had happened, she was already gone. I must have interrupted her while she was leaving the wine and my other little present." She indicated the pâté. "I know I locked the door before I left."

"How about the window?" I asked, checking the latch on the open window. It appeared to be unmolested.

Allison looked crestfallen. "I didn't think to check. I mean, I did have it open earlier, but I thought I shut it. I'm not sure." After a moment, she chuckled. "I don't think I'll be trying the pâté. What do you think?"

The pâté in question was heaped in a small oval mound in the center of the plate, accompanied by a butter knife and a dozen Ritz crackers. In front of the plate was a brief note. I looked at Allison in surprise. The note read, "For Allison, from Cassidy."

"Obviously, they wanted me to think it was from you," she said.

"Whoever it is, they sure as hell moved quickly. My name on the card must've been a last-minute thought. A nice little added touch."

She bent over to sniff the pâté.

"Allison, don't." I pulled her back. "It could be poisoned. Depending on what was used, it could be dangerous just to inhale it. I'm going to bag it."

I found a plastic Baggie and dumped the pâte, plate and all, inside. I sealed it with a twist tie and carried it into my room, putting it in the back of the refrigerator. Somehow, I'd need to get it back to Portland for an analysis. Otherwise, we'd never know for sure. But I'd seen a tin of pâte in my own refrigerator, and I knew it didn't come shaped in that mound. Obviously, someone had re-shaped it on the plate. Probably after adding a few ingredients, I thought.

"They didn't waste much time, did they?" Her voice was so vulnerable, all my earlier anger dissipated.

"There's something we need to look at," I said. My heart was beating rapidly. Could it be this easy? Was I really going to be able to break the case on the very first night? I took her into my closet and showed her the camera.

"You videotaped my room?" she said. "Were you planning on telling me?"

I ignored this and hit the rewind button. I flipped the little screen on the side of the camera to face us and hit the play button. I remembered, but too late. Allison's face appeared on the screen, and then the camera's angle widened so that her whole body was facing it. Her robe dropped, and there she stood, pale skin glistening from the heat of the spa. I closed my eyes, wishing I could disappear. The image of her erect nipples was still etched clearly in my mind. The screen went suddenly black and then came back on.

"You were watching me?" she asked. I was glad I

couldn't see her face beside me in the dark closet. I was glad she couldn't see mine.

"I was trying to get the camera angle right when you walked in. I didn't know you were going to drop your robe. Honest."

"I notice you didn't bother to rewind it, though." I couldn't tell if she was angry or amused. I was mortified.

We sat in silence, crouched in the closet, staring at the screen. Whenever the motion sensor had picked up movement, the camera had caught the action. Unfortunately, the last action it caught was Allison flinging a red shirt into the closet right before we'd left for dinner. The shirt covered the hole, rendering the camera blind. I sighed and punched the rewind button. If only I'd told her, we'd have her attacker on tape.

I could tell that Allison was upset too, but she was being a good sport about it. "Well, it's not a total loss," she said. I looked at her, puzzled. "We at least got a decent bottle of wine out of it. Come on, let's open it. She can't have poisoned a sealed bottle. Let's go out to the spa. My shoulder's killing me."

"Well, I guess it isn't too likely she'll try twice in one night," I conceded. "But she might just come back to clear the evidence. Let me put another tape in, and then we can go."

The moon shed enough light for us to see our way to the back without the flashlights the lodge had thoughtfully provided. To my surprise, the hot tub was not directly behind the cabin as I'd expected.

"Come on, it's up here." Allison led me up some cedar stairs dug into the hill and as we climbed, the smell of sulphur grew stronger. Finally, we came to a clearing in the trees. There, completely protected from prying eyes, was our own private spa. Steam rose in great puffs of white from the dark water.

"Look away," I said, slipping out of my robe.

"Oh, right. After you videotaped me nude you want me to look away?" But she did, and moaning aloud, I sank into the wonderfully hot water.

"That horse really gave you a ride, eh?" She climbed into the tub, and I studied the sky.

"I was lucky just to hang on. Damn thing nearly broke my back."

"Want me to rub it?" she asked.

"No." I added, more softly, "But thanks."

Allison laughed. "You really are afraid of me, aren't you? If I give you my word of honor that I won't try to seduce you, will you relax?"

She handed me a glass and I took a sip of the dry but pleasantly fruity wine. It was the same red we'd had with dinner and I wondered if Allison's attacker had lifted a bottle from one of the tables. Through the trees we could see glimpses of the lake and the snowy peak of Mount Hood in the distance. The sky was studded with a brilliant splash of stars. The night air was chilly, but the hot water was thoroughly relaxing.

"Maybe that was fourth down and now they'll give up," she said, sinking her sore shoulder below the water. I sighed. We both knew it wasn't very likely. We gazed again at the stars.

"She didn't leave a note," I said.

"The notes have always come later, though. She's probably composing one as we speak."

"Hmmm."

"What?" Allison asked.

"I was just thinking. If the pâté is poisoned, it fits the stalker's m.o. But hitting you with the bottle is a new twist. It could be she's getting more brazen."

"It could be she wasn't expecting me to come in the door just then, too. You have any idea who it is yet?"

"Who do *you* think it is?"

"Not Billie."

"I admit, I like her too. But I can't rule anyone out. Any one of them could have seen us walk down to the lake and figured they had enough time to drop off the pâté."

"I don't think it's Lacy either."

"She does seem quite taken with you. Were you lovers?"

"She'd like to be, but no, we've never been lovers. This may sound vain, but I think Lacy idolizes me too much. It wouldn't be right. She has spent the night at my house, but our relationship is purely platonic."

"I didn't know you were so discriminating." This was a lousy thing to say and I knew it. When she didn't answer, I felt terrible. "Allison, I'm sorry. That was uncalled for."

She pinned me down with a hard stare. "Yes, it was," she said. "As long as you don't make a habit of it. I'm not fond of mean-spirited people." She smiled then, and we both relaxed.

"Like Reeva?"

"Reeva's mostly bluster. She's really very insecure. She'd like more power because she truly believes that her ideas are the right way. She knows that she rubs people the wrong way, and she'd never get enough votes to be president. She resents my popularity."

"I assume that if you were dead, she'd be president in your place. Maybe she's figured out the only way she'll ever *be* president is if that happens."

"But there'll be a new election next year. One year's not very long. And besides, like I told you, Reeva probably doesn't even know I drink milk or that my driveway goes right out onto a highway. She's never been to my house. At least not by invitation."

"But maybe she got that information from someone else," I offered. Or maybe she's been stalking you, I thought. Aloud I said, "Did she know you were allergic to bees?"

"She could have, but she doesn't have a key to my house. As much as I don't trust Reeva, I don't think she's the one."

I shrugged noncommittally. In truth, I didn't trust Reeva at all. And although I had started concocting motives for the other women, I still thought Reeva's motive was worth pursuing.

"Allie," I said, wondering why the nickname had tumbled out, "who gets your money when you die?"

She stood up to pour us more wine. She seemed unconcerned with exposing her breasts, and after all, I had already seen them. Still, I couldn't help an admiring glance. I immediately turned toward the lake.

"The organization. I've willed Women On Top my entire estate." She handed me my glass and slid back into the water.

"You're kidding, right?" When she shook her head,

I took a deep breath. "And how many people know this?"

"Just my attorney, Kate Monroe, as far as I know. Then again, she was Holly's lover, off and on last year, so I suppose it's possible Holly knows. But she's never said anything to me about it. As the financial advisor for Women On Top, Holly's aware that on a few occasions I've made a personal donation. It's not something I want others to know and she respects that."

"Jesus, Allison. You're telling me that the group's financial advisor and your own attorney were sleeping together and it never dawned on you that this might be about money?" I'd forgotten my earlier modesty and was standing in the tub. "How much, exactly, if I might ask, is your estate worth?"

"Including my inheritance, about two million I'd guess."

I stared at her, open-mouthed.

"My great-grandfather was Sebastian Crane, the boat manufacturer. There was a lot more money at one time, from what I understand, but my dear old dad managed to gamble most of it away. Before he drove his T-Bird off a bridge, killing my mother and himself in the process. Not intentionally, so they say. But there was no other car involved, so who knows? Anyway, that's ancient history. Most of the two million is from a trust fund my father couldn't touch. I haven't touched it much myself, for that matter. It's just sitting there collecting interest."

"And you never considered that this might be worth mentioning?" My voice had risen at least an octave.

"I like Holly," she said, starting to pout. "I'm pretty sure she likes me. I can't believe she'd try to kill me just to get her hands on the money willed to Women On Top. It's not like she could take it for herself."

No, not outright, I thought, but she could sure manipulate where it ended up. With Allison out of the picture, who would know how much money was being funneled into which accounts? Especially if the only other person aware of Allison's fortune was Holly's ex. They could well be in this together.

"Is Holly your personal financial advisor as well?" I asked, getting out of the tub.

"No. Just for Women On Top. Where are you going?" Allison was scrambling out behind me.

"To check the tape," I said. "And to do some thinking. Right now, I just want to think."

Chapter Eight

In the dream, the creature was cloaked in darkness. Murky water obscured its features, but somehow I could make out the eyes. They were bathed in hatred. I knew I needed to see the thing's face, but doing so would necessitate diving deeper into the dark waters. And I needed to get to the surface or I'd drown. I kicked out, trying to get free, and found myself on the floor. I'd rolled off the damn bed.

It was early Tuesday morning and the birds were chirping merrily away. I could tell it was going to be another beautiful day. My thighs were stiff from yesterday's ride, but other than that, I felt fine. What I needed was a good long walk and some breakfast.

I listened at Allison's door and heard nothing. Feeling guilty, I went into the closet and peered through the view-finder. We'd moved the offending red shirt the night before and I had a clear shot of most of the room. She was safe in bed, sleeping soundly. I doubted her assailant would try anything so early in the morning, so I slipped into a pair of sweats and quietly let myself out of the cabin.

I wasn't the only early riser that morning. A few couples strolled along the lakeshore, and now and then I passed a jogger, but for the most part the resort was quiet. I liked it this way. In fact, I wouldn't have minded bringing Maggie up here sometime when there weren't a hundred other women. I forced myself to concentrate on the case, wishing I knew which cabins the other staff members were in. I made my way to the lodge and wasn't surprised to see Stella, the turquoise-lover, already watering flowerpots on the front deck.

"There's coffee inside, if you're interested."

"Actually, I was wondering if you could help me locate some friends of mine. I mean, I know they're here, I just don't know which cabins they're in."

"Register's right on the desk there, if you wanna take a look-see. Help yourself." I could've kissed her then and there.

I searched around for something to write with and jotted down the cabin names as I found them. Now all I needed was to locate the cabins themselves. I took one of the maps lying on the counter and went back out to talk with Stella.

"I don't suppose you have a fax machine?"

"Up here? We don't even got a phone." She laughed. "We keep all the fancy gadgets down at the T-Bone. That's where all our business is conducted. Up here, we keep things simple. Some folks find it inconvenient but it suits me fine." She paused, seeming to realize that I was probably one of the ones who found it inconvenient. "I can radio down for you, or if you want, Buddy can send a fax out. He goes down for supplies every morning. But you better hurry if you want to catch him this morning. He's probably already saddled up."

I ran back inside and made a hasty note to Martha at the precinct, asking her to do a background check on the WOT staff members. I jotted down their names and ran to the corrals in search of Buddy. I found him saddling a gray gelding.

"Can you fax this for me?" I asked, handing him the folded slip of paper. He unfolded it and started reading. "It's kind of confidential," I said.

His freckled face turned pink. "Oh, sorry." He refolded it and stuffed it in his shirt pocket.

"The fax number's on the front there, but you'll need to write the T-Bone Ranch fax number on the inside before you send it or they won't know where to send the return message."

"You want me to bring you an answer?" He didn't look too happy about it.

"It sure would be helpful," I said. "It could take them a while to get what I need, though. Could you just check the fax machine before you come back up? I'd really appreciate it." I flashed him a smile and he shrugged, pulling himself up onto the horse.

"You're the one that nearly got throwed off of Diablo, ain't you?" He peered at me more closely and

I nodded. "Well, I guess I do sorta owe you one, then. I'll send this off first thing and check for an answer before I head on back up here this afternoon."

I thanked him and walked back toward the lodge, hoping that Martha would be able to find something useful. I knew I'd owe her something really gourmet for this favor, but I felt like I was operating in the dark up here. At the very least she should be able to tell me if any of the women had a criminal record. Knowing Martha, she'd go the extra mile and find out more than that, provided she didn't have the day off or was out of the office. In the meantime, maybe searching the cabins would prove fruitful, I thought, studying the map.

The first thing I noticed was that Lacy Watkins and Sabrina Pepper had a suite similar to Allison's and mine, and in the same general area. Holly and Fay's cabins were fairly close to ours too, while Reeva's, Billie's and Karen's were all on the opposite end of the resort's grounds. If any one of the three had left what I assumed was poisoned pâte in Allison's cabin, she would've had to haul some pretty serious ass to get all the way back to her cabin, retrieve the poisoned goods, run all the way to our suite, crawl through the window, and hope to make it back to the lodge before anyone noticed her missing. It was probably do-able, but it would've been a heck of a lot easier for Lacy, Sabrina, Fay or Holly to pull it off.

And how did any of them know the window would be unlocked in the first place? Unless they'd either seen it earlier or had sneaked in and unlatched it themselves. Given Allison's propensity for hot-tubbing, that seemed an easy enough task.

Suddenly, another thought hit me. Whoever it was had to know that Allison and I were suite-mates. They must have known it before we even pretended to be introduced, because otherwise, how would I have supposedly gotten into Allison's cabin to leave the wine and pâte? Like me, the stalker must have checked Stella's guest list. When she saw that Allison and I hit it off during dinner, her mind must have gone into overdrive.

From the outside, most of the cabins looked quiet, although smoke curled out of a few chimneys, and now and then I caught the aroma of someone cooking breakfast. I noticed Billie's curtains were pulled open, so maybe she was up, but Karen's and Reeva's cabins were dark and silent. Heading back to my cabin to see if Sleeping Beauty was still sacked out, I nearly bumped into Sabrina Pepper coming around the bend.

"You're up early," she said, a tight smile on her thin lips. She was a slender, pale woman, with light blue eyes and fine straw-colored hair that flipped up at her shoulders. Her bangs were so long they must have obscured her vision; she had a habit of blowing upward to keep them out of her eyes. It would have been easier to get a trim, I thought, returning her smile.

"It's so beautiful up here, I didn't want to waste any of the day by sleeping in. How about you? You always an early riser?"

"Not always. I just felt like getting out, that's all. I'm surprised that after last night you're not exhausted." Her cheeks had taken on a faint blush, and although her lips were smiling, her eyes were not.

"I'm not sure what you mean," I said, knowing exactly what she meant. Apparently, people had taken note of Allison's and my early departure.

"Huh!" She sounded as young as she looked, which was about fourteen, and I guessed she was probably in her thirties. "I'm not stupid, you know," she said, crossing her arms. Her eyes challenged me to refute this.

"Sabrina, have I done something to offend you? If I have, I assure you, it was unintentional."

"Of course not." She exhaled and suddenly she looked sad. "Anyway, it's not you. Forget I said anything. You haven't done anything wrong. If I were as pretty as you, I'd be flirting with Allison too. Just don't get your hopes up."

"You're kidding, right?"

She stared back at me with baleful eyes and I realized she was serious. Was it possible she didn't know how attractive she really was? Like anorexics who forever see themselves as overweight, did Sabrina see herself as homely? She tugged at her earlobe self-consciously, squirming under my scrutiny.

"I take it you and Allison have dated?"

Her eyes grew wide, as if I'd slapped her. Her blush deepened. She nodded.

"I'm sorry. I didn't know. If I'm out of line, just tell me."

"It's over," she said. "I don't know why I get so crazy every time she dates someone else. I should be used to it by now."

"How long ago did you break up?" I asked.

Sabrina's laugh surprised me. It was high and thin, like a misplayed note on a flute. "No one ever breaks up with Allison. She just sort of moves on. Anyway, like I said, I should be over it by now. Please, don't let my little emotional outburst get in the way of your affair."

"For what it's worth," I said, "it hasn't exactly come to that."

Sabrina's eyes brightened. "You haven't slept together?" She sounded incredulous.

"I just met her last night." I felt oddly defensive.

"Yeah, but. Well. Hmm." I could practically see her mind wrestling with this unexpected news. She seemed unduly cheered. Then her brow furrowed. "But you want to, right?" She watched me expectantly. I felt my own face blush at this candid question. "I'm sorry. That's none of my business. Forget I asked, okay? God, I can't believe I even said that. I'm not normally this forward." She'd turned suddenly loquacious and full of vitality. This woman had more mood swings than I could keep up with. "Guess I'll see you at breakfast," she said, practically skipping away.

Walking back toward the cabin, I felt as though I'd just come through a whirlwind and wasn't sure I still had everything intact. Sabrina Pepper was a bundle of contradictions. But was she crazy enough to be a killer?

Allison was not only up but dressed and sitting out on the front deck with a cup of coffee. "Grab a cup and come join me," she called over the wall that divided our porches. I walked through our adjoining doors and helped myself to a cup of coffee from her kitchen, then joined her on the deck.

"I just had an interesting chat with one of your many exes," I said, sitting down beside her.

"Is that jealousy I detect?" Her aqua eyes were dancing.

"Very funny. Tell me about Sabrina Pepper."

Allison smiled, looking pensive. "Sabrina's a real sweetheart, but she gives too much of herself and ends up getting hurt. I think she tries to buy people's love, which is sad, because they'd give it freely. Her ego is so frail. She doesn't acknowledge her own self-worth."

"She seems pretty hung up on you," I pointed out.

"I try not to encourage her," Allison said. "When I realized she was really falling for me, I tried to ease off gently. Maybe too gently. Sometimes I think she's just waiting for me to change my mind."

"The jilted lover has been known to seek revenge," I stated mildly.

Allison looked up, startled. "You think Sabrina's the one?"

"She does seem kind of unbalanced."

"But she likes me!" Allison said.

"*Like* isn't really the word I'd use. *Fixated* is more like it."

"God, I'd hate for it to be Sabrina." She stood up and started pacing the deck.

"Who would you like it to be?"

This brought her back to her chair. She slumped into it, drawing her knees to her chin. "I'd like it to be over, is what I'd like. Damn. What are you going to do?"

Like Sabrina, Allison had an amazing ability to shift moods. She'd just gone from carefree and cocky to scared and vulnerable. I wasn't sure which way I liked her best.

"Well, first I'm going to do some nosing around after breakfast while you hold your staff meeting. Do you think you can keep your meeting running an hour?"

"It'll be at least that long. More likely an hour and a half. We have a lot to do. But be careful, Cass. There aren't any workshops scheduled until tomorrow so there'll be a lot of people out and about. Someone might see you."

"I'll be careful. It's you I'm worried about. Although I assume you'll be safe as long as you're in a group. Unless, of course, they're all in it together." I smiled sweetly, and Allison laughed.

"Thank you very much. That's one possibility I hadn't even considered until now. My dreams should be really great tonight."

"You having nightmares?"

"Only when I sleep. Which isn't much."

"Join the crowd."

"Nightmares or not sleeping?"

"I've been having this dream," I said, not sure why I was telling her. "It's been a few weeks now, before we even met. But I can't help thinking it's got something to do with this case. A premonition, sort of. Only I can't figure out what it means. Something evil is trying to drag me down into the lake. I never see its face but I know it's bad. I'm drowning, struggling to get to the surface for air. I kick and kick, trying to get free. Just as I'm ready to draw my last breath, one I know will draw water into my lungs, I wake up. This morning, I kicked so hard, I found myself on the floor."

"Does this happen often? Your having premonitions?"

"Not like this."

"Maybe if you could get a look at the face, you'd know who was trying to kill me."

"In the dream, the only way I'd be able to see the face, is if I went down with it. And if I did that, I'd drown."

"Hmm. You want some more coffee?"

When she came back, I was so absorbed in thought, I didn't hear her. She put her hand on my shoulder to let me know she was behind me and the touch was so light it sent shivers right up my neck.

"Sorry. I didn't mean to startle you."

"After breakfast, try to keep them for that hour and a half," I said gruffly, standing up. I was miffed at the unwanted goosebumps.

"Whose cabin are you checking?" she asked.

"All seven of them, if I can. Starting with Reeva's and Karen's, since they're the farthest away. I'll work my way back here, hopefully before you finish."

"What will you be looking for?" she asked.

I sighed. I had no idea.

Chapter Nine

The dining room was much less crowded for breakfast and was set up buffet-style. I sat with Allison and Billie, enjoying Billie's account of a camping trip they'd made in which Reeva had gotten locked in the outhouse. We were still laughing when Lacy and Sabrina joined us.

"How are you two enjoying your suite?" Lacy asked. She was wearing hot pink shorts and a matching top. Her brown curly hair framed her dimpled cheeks, and despite her rather noticeable overbite, she was cute. She sort of reminded me of

Shirley Temple, and the way she bounced on her chair made me think she was on the verge of breaking into song and dance. I glanced at her, wondering how she knew Allison and I had a suite, but her bright, hazel eyes revealed nothing more than healthy curiosity.

"It's in a nice location," I offered.

"Sabrina and I are just down the hill from you. Ours doesn't have quite the privacy of yours, but it's in a real sunny spot. I like the suites better than the single cabins. As long as you're not sharing with a bathroom hog." She smiled her buck-toothed grin at Sabrina, who seemed shy after our talk on the trail. She was pushing around a small mound of scrambled eggs with her fork, occasionally nibbling at a piece of toast.

"You going to enter the race?" Allison asked. Lacy nodded enthusiastically but Sabrina just shrugged. "You should enter," she said, clearly trying to cajole Sabrina out of her shyness. "With your sailing skills, you could win it!"

"What race is that?" I asked.

"It's a lot of fun," Lacy volunteered. "You should sign up. It's not till Thursday, but there's limited space to enter. It's sort of a camp tradition. A triathalon with a twist." When I looked puzzled, she giggled. "First you get a vest with an emblem on it. It could be a star, a moon, a four-leaf clover or any number of things. You gotta wear it the whole time. The first part of the race is on foot. It starts at the lodge and goes down to the pier. A little more than a mile, I'd say. Anyway, at the pier, you've gotta find the sailboat with your emblem on the sail. The same one that's on your vest. That's your boat. You sail over to the island, pull up on the beach, and look for the flag with your emblem. They're hidden all over the island, but they have to be in plain sight. You're not allowed to take or move anyone else's flag. When you find yours, you take it back to your boat, sail back to the pier, and race to the finish line. It's really a hoot!"

"Sounds fun," I said.

"Too much luck and too little skill," Reeva said, sitting down across from Sabrina. Her yellow flattop was still wet from the shower. "Some of the sailboats are faster than others. If you get a slow one, you don't stand a chance."

"Or if someone moves your flag," Sabrina said, nodding.

"They're not allowed to do that," Lacy said, plucking a piece of bacon from Reeva's plate and crunching into it.

"Hey!" Reeva made a feigned attempt at Lacy's wrist with her fork.

"People do cheat," Sabrina said, blue eyes narrowing.

"I don't think that's a real big threat in this group. It's just for fun," Allison said.

"Me, I'd rather compete in something more straightforward. Like archery. Or football."

"Oh Reeva, you're so predictable," Lacy said. Reeva looked as if Lacy had slapped her.

"She's a Seahawks fanatic," Lacy said to me. "The only thing she'd rather be doing than watching football is playing it."

"I'd have made the varsity if they'd have let me try out," Reeva said. "Still ticks me off they wouldn't even give me a shot at it."

"There's a girl place-kicker in Eugene," Karen said, joining us. She mussed Reeva's flattop and winked at me across the table. "She hasn't missed a single field goal in two years."

"Reeva wanted to play quarterback in high school," Sabrina explained.

"I'd have settled for linebacker. Hell, I'd have kicked the damn ball. I just wanted a chance to play."

"Maybe we can toss the ball around later, get a little pick-up game going," Lacy said, finally realizing she'd hurt Reeva's feelings.

"Yeah, a little touch football. We'll make it a picnic!" Allison was getting into the mood.

"Touch football with a bunch of women just ain't the same," Reeva grumbled. But her eyes had lit up at the prospect and I saw Billie and Allison exchange relieved glances. I got the feeling no one wanted to see Reeva in a bad mood.

Holly McIntyre and Fay Daniels were the last to arrive, and I couldn't help thinking of Mutt and Jeff. Holly had obviously spent hours doing her Farrah Fawcett hair and she was dressed to the nines. Fay wore an ancient tattered gray sweatshirt over faded jeans and looked like someone who'd never spent more than half a minute in front of a mirror. Her epic ponytail was the only evidence that somewhere beneath the bland exterior lay a tiny spark of vanity. I watched as she placed a wedge of melon, a banana and half of a dry bagel on her plate before sitting down.

"Don't you want some cream cheese at least?" Lacy asked, wrinkling her nose at the healthy diet.

Fay, obviously not a morning person, just smiled and shrugged, biting into the banana.

"Looks like we're going to have to make you an honorary member," Holly said, shooting me a conspiratorial grin.

"I was just leaving," I said. "Business meetings are not my thing."

"Mine neither," Reeva grumbled.

"I second that!" Karen said. I left chuckling over the constant bickering that seemed to permeate their every conversation. Like some big families, they seemed to thrive on sparring. Personally, I preferred more peace and quiet, and was glad to get outside.

The grounds weren't as deserted as I'd hoped, but it probably wasn't ever going to get any better. I started with Reeva Dunsmoore's cabin, which was the farthest away from mine. I'd brought my lock picks with me but Reeva's door was unlocked. I waited for a group of women to pass, then turned the knob and stepped inside.

Reeva hadn't made her bed, nor had she picked up her clothes. I did a quick look around and then, feeling guilty, went straight for her suitcase. The only thing of interest amid the underwear, T-shirts, jeans and flannels was a Swiss Army knife. Not that it meant anything, but if she had one, it was a good thing for me to know.

As I continued my search, I was careful to put things back as I'd found them. I went through her bathroom, but there wasn't much of interest there. Her kitchen trashcan was full of beer cans, for the most part, but also signs that she'd had a few snacks from the well-stocked kitchen. There was no pâté tin in the trash but when I searched the fridge and cupboard I couldn't find an unopened one either. Just because I had a tin of pâté in my kitchen, and Allison had one in hers, didn't necessarily mean that every kitchen was stocked with the exact same items. On the other hand, if there had been a tin of pâté to start with, there wasn't one now. Maybe Stella could enlighten me as to how the cabins were stocked.

Feeling like I was spending too much time in Reeva's cabin, I quickly let myself out and headed for Billie's. I hadn't enjoyed going through Reeva's things and for some reason the prospect of violating Billie's privacy bothered me even more. I supposed I didn't want to believe that someone I liked was trying to kill Allison. But I'd never forgive myself if the one cabin I skipped turned out to be the assailant's. After waiting for a couple to stroll by, I stepped onto her porch and tried the door. Like Reeva's, it was unlocked and I let myself inside.

Billie's cabin was neater than Reeva's. She'd picked wild flowers and placed them on the kitchenette table. Her curtains were wide open, which made the room quite bright but also meant that anyone passing by could see me prowling around. She'd put her clothes into the small drawers in the nightstand, and the rest were hung in the closet. Her tastes ran from flashy to wild, with lots of oranges and reds. Even her underwear were the french-cut silky kind.

Her bed was made, and as I'd done in Reeva's room, I looked under the bed and checked under the pillows. The only thing I found was an expensive

Nikon camera in a leather case. There was an opened bottle of chardonnay on the counter, corked with just a glassful missing. One wine glass sat upside down in the dish drainer on the counter. When I opened her refrigerator I found not one, but two tins of pâte. I also noticed that she had a small jar of lumpfish caviar, something I'd not found in my own refrigerator. I was beginning to think that the notion of finding the killer by seeing who didn't have pâte was a lost cause. The only thing of real interest in the whole cabin was that underneath the kitchen sink, I found a partially full container of rat poison. I hadn't taken the time to look under Reeva's sink. In fact, I'd never even looked under my own. I wondered if all the cabins had rat poison. And I wondered what rat poison would taste like.

Outside, I checked my watch and knew that it was probably going to be impossible to look at all seven cabins. Karen Castillo's was next on my list, and I walked as quickly as I could. Between the women who'd opted to skip breakfast and those who'd just tumbled out of bed, the place was starting to become uncomfortably less deserted. Women were milling around, and sneaking in was becoming tricky. I pretended to tie my shoelaces as a woman jogged by, then quickly tried Karen's door. It was locked. I fumbled with my picks until I heard the satisfying click of the simple mechanism and the knob turned in my palm.

When I got inside, I was struck by how neat everything looked. The bed was made up military-style with hospital corners and there wasn't a single wrinkle in the spread. I checked under the pillow and was careful to place it back exactly as I'd found it.

Under the bed I found a suitcase, the clothes inside folded with such precision, I was afraid to disturb them. I cautiously slid my hand underneath the clothes and when my hand bumped against something hard, my heart quickened.

Slowly, I slid the object out. It was a lady's wallet. Aside from a hundred and twenty three dollars, there were two gas company credit cards, a Visa and an American Express card, each neatly encased in a plastic sheath. There was a photo compartment with four pictures which I found interesting. One was of Karen in the classroom, her arm around two boys in front of the chalkboard. On the board was a chart of what looked like the periodic tables. Another photo was similar to one Allison had shown me of the WOT staff standing behind a snowman. Lacy had locked arms with Holly and both were laughing. Reeva had her arms crossed in front of her, her tongue stuck out at the camera. Sabrina, smiling shyly, had one arm around Karen, the other around someone who'd been cut out of the picture. I knew from having seen Allison's print, that it was Allison who'd been excised. The only people missing were Billie, who must have taken the picture, and Fay, who hadn't been part of the group yet.

I felt my pulse quicken, staring at the altered photo. This could be my first real clue. Why would Karen cut Allison's picture out of the group shot? The other two prints were of a big, black Labrador, yellow eyes gleaming at the camera.

There was no pâte in Karen's refrigerator, and since her trash had been emptied, there was no way of knowing if there ever had been. Just as at Billie's, there was a partially full container of rat poison under the sink. As I let myself out the door, I was still kicking myself for not having looked under Reeva's sink.

I'd spent too much time looking through Karen's wallet, and had to jog past the lodge toward the other cabins. Women were now out in increasing numbers, and a few looked up and smiled as I passed. I tried to look like I was out for the exercise rather than in a hurry, but my heart was racing. When I reached the next cabin, I had to waste several minutes before I could safely approach the door.

Sabrina and Lacy's suite was almost identical to ours. I let myself into Sabrina's side, checking my watch. I only had about twenty minutes before Allison's ninety minutes were up.

Sabrina's curtains were closed, which was a relief, considering all the women out and about. I did a quick glance through her closet and drawers, surprised to find a book tucked away beneath her underwear. Holding my breath, I flipped through the pages, hoping I'd found her diary. But each page, although penned in her own tiny scrawl, was filled with nothing but poetry. It was depressing stuff. It made Sylvia Plath sound cheerful.

The clouds, though they seem nonchalant,
are watching, waiting, lurking near,
they follow me, their bellies black,
like hounds they sniff the air for fear.

On another page:

Should I slit them down or up,
or maybe straight across?
And who will notice, who will care,
when all the blood is lost?

I put the book back, suddenly burdened by the desperation and hopelessness in her words. I felt myself moving more slowly than I should have and forced myself to snap out of it.

There was no pâte in Sabrina's refrigerator, but lo and behold, there was at last an empty container in her trash can! Even better, there was a partially empty box of Ritz crackers in the cupboard. I hadn't thought to check for crackers in the other cabins, but this was promising. Of course, if someone checked my cabin, they'd find that my own box of Ritz crackers was partially empty.

There was no rat poison under her sink. Had she used up the rest of her rat poison in the pâte, and then taken it to Allison's cabin? If so, what had she done with the container of poison? And most of all, had the pâte even been poisoned in the first place? I was operating on the assumption that it had been, but I knew it was just as possible that I was wrong. Besides, rat poison wasn't the only common poison. The normal household was full of deadly concoctions. These cabins probably were too.

I had no time to mull any of this over. My time was almost up. I went through the adjoining bathroom, taking a quick look in the medicine cabinet. I was surprised by the array of medications lined up on the shelf. Some were prescription drugs with

Sabrina's name on them. At least she was getting help for her depression, I thought, studying the labels. But I wondered what kind of doctor would prescribe so many things at once. Surely, if she were taking Prozac, she shouldn't also need Valium. There was also an impressive assortment of vitamins, which I didn't have time to look at. I slipped into Lacy's room, intent on giving it at least a quick once-over before making my escape. I knew there was no way I'd have time to see both Holly's and Fay's cabins too.

Lacy's room was a cross between Karen's ultra-tidiness and Reeva's complete disarray. Whereas Lacy had pulled up the bedspread, she hadn't bothered to smooth the blankets and sheets beneath it, so it appeared lumpy. There were no clothes strewn around the room, but when I opened the closet, they were piled on the floor. Lacy apparently was a slob who didn't want other people to know it. I couldn't find signs of any pâte, but I did notice a pretty full box of the rat poison, along with a mouse trap under the sink. The resort must be crawling with rodents, I thought, heading for the door.

At the last second, I paused to look under Lacy's bed and pillow. To my surprise, I actually felt a hard lump inside the pillowcase. Another diary? My heart surged. I pulled out what to my surprise and disappointment turned out to be nothing more than a Bible. I slipped it back inside the pillowcase, wondering why she'd hidden it, and let myself out.

By now, the grounds were virtually crawling with people as the bus bearing the new arrivals had finally made it up the mountain. I jogged toward the last two cabins knowing I probably wouldn't have time to search both. I was more interested in Holly's, but Fay's was closer.

After a bit of artful dodging, I approached Fay's door and knocked several times to make sure she was gone. The door was locked, so once again, I went to work with my picks.

Fay's room was almost as tidy as Karen's. Her clothes, a mundane collection of faded sweats and jeans, were loosely stacked in piles on the closet shelf and it didn't appear as though Fay had bought herself a new outfit in twenty years.

On the nightstand next to the bed I found an old Army T-shirt that was so thin I could almost see through it. Someone had used a black marker to print a name on the label and I wondered who F. Anderson was. Did Fay wear someone else's old T-shirt to bed at night? Or did the F stand for Fay herself? She was certainly neat enough to have been in the Army, I thought. If the shirt was hers, her name must have been Anderson at one time. Had Fay been married?

There was a pocket-sized computerized chess game in the nightstand drawer, testimony to her reclusive nature, but there was nothing at all that led me to believe she was involved in Allison's situation. Sighing, I let myself out of the cabin, knowing I'd pushed my luck time-wise. The moment I stepped out the door, I saw them coming.

Sabrina, Allison, Holly, Fay and Lacy walked straight toward me up the path and I felt my pulse quicken as I scrambled for an explanation.

"Out for another walk?" Sabrina asked, blowing the blond bangs off her forehead.

"Trying to walk off that breakfast," I improvised. "How'd your meeting go?"

They exchanged glances and Holly rolled her eyes. "Same ol', same ol'. We can't agree, so we agree to disagree. Which means about six hundred more meetings. Reeva wants us to turn our back on the Democratic Party until they start backing us. Allison says we'll lose what little support we have. It goes 'round and 'round."

"So what's new?" Lacy said, bouncing on the balls of her feet. "Reeva not only wants to bite the hand that feeds her, she thinks anyone else who doesn't is a coward."

"She's just more committed than some of us," Sabrina said. She seemed surprised she'd spoken and hugged her sweater around her.

"Reeva has some good points," Allison said. "There's room in this organization for dissenting points of view."

"Allison's just being magnanimous," Lacy said, flashing me a full-toothed grin. "She knows Reeva's a pain."

"She's not a pain," Sabrina insisted, her pale cheeks coloring. "She just doesn't express her ideas as well as some people."

I was beginning to wish I hadn't asked.

"Aren't you glad you didn't stick around?" Holly asked, as if reading my mind. "Hang out with this group long enough, we'll almost start to seem normal." She shot me a conspiratorial wink.

We were standing just outside Fay's cabin in a

patch of sun. It was mid-morning, and the air was thick with pine scent. Blue jays quarreled above us and the ever present roar of a waterfall could be heard in the distance. If only Maggie were with me, I'd have loved to spend the day exploring the surrounding forest. Allison must have seen the look in my eyes.

"Wait till you see where we're going for lunch," she said. Sabrina shot her a hurt glance, but Allison seemed oblivious.

"It's about the only thing anyone could agree on," Fay added. A small smile played at her mouth but disappeared quickly, as if she were afraid someone might think she was being critical. I was beginning to think that her silent act had more to do with shyness than a lack of something to say.

"Aside from the island, it's my favorite spot up here," Lacy said. "Best place in the world for a picnic. But you've got to bring something decadent if you're going to join us. And I've already got dibs on mini-mart brownies."

"Of course she's going to join us," Holly said. "Aren't you?"

Sabrina's eyes were smoldering.

"I don't want to crash a private party. I mean, if it's business, you don't need someone hanging around..."

"We've had enough business for one day. This is purely pleasure." Holly regarded me with humor. She too must have caught Sabrina's reaction to Allison's inviting me along. I got the feeling Holly was enjoying the interaction.

We went our separate ways, with plans to meet at

the base of the hiking trail at eleven-thirty. I walked
Allison back to her cabin, checking first to make sure
all was safe inside. Then I let myself into my place
through the bathroom and told Allison to let me
know if she went out. She assured me that after so
many sleepless nights, all she wanted was to take a
brief nap.

Even so, I checked the camera to make sure
nothing obscured the view and then, knowing I often
did my best thinking in the kitchen, went straight
for the fridge.

I rummaged around, deciding pâte was definitely
out. I found a jar of green, pimento-stuffed olives, a
slab of cheddar and some Bisquick. Improvising, I
made up a cheddar dough and rolled it into quarter-
sized balls, inserting an olive into each round. This
gave me an idea, so I searched the cupboards for
other things to wrap in the dough. Vienna sausage?
Why not? Sardines? Definitely out. I found a can of
nuts and folded almonds and cashews into the cheese
dough, laughing at my weird sense of adventure.
When at last I ran out of dough, I slid the "cheese
balls" into the oven and hoped for the best. Ten
minutes later, they were puffed and golden. Satisfied,
I cleaned up the kitchen, then got to work.

I started by making a chart of what I knew. I
made a brief character sketch of each woman,
followed by possible motives, relationships to Allison,
particular talents and skills, observable eccentricities
and general behavior patterns. I drew lines connecting the women, with explanations of how they
related to one another. My hand was starting to
cramp when Allison knocked on my door, telling me

it was time to go. I looked at what I'd written and shook my head. Two things were clear: Allison had surrounded herself with an interesting assortment of oddballs, and I was no closer to knowing which one of them wanted to kill her.

Chapter Ten

I was surprised, and in truth a bit relieved, to see that the group at the base of the trail included others besides the staff of Women On Top. Billie had brought the woman staying in the cabin next to hers. Peaches was a short, heavy-set computer analyst in her early twenties, who giggled nervously upon being introduced. Reeva brought her dance partner from the night before, Harriet, a slender, feminine Asian wearing a midriff and pink bicycle shorts with a gold hoop protruding from her navel. With Karen was another couple who'd come all the way from Arizona to vacation at the resort. They were an attractive, athletic pair in their fifties and looked enough alike to be sisters. They were both in real estate and I hoped to God neither of them asked me about the Oregon market.

The trail wound through the forest, lacy trees arching overhead, occasional streams crossing our path. As we climbed, the sound of the waterfall grew louder. The forest floor was lush with wild mushrooms sprouting out of fallen logs, and fat robins hopped through the wildflowers searching for worms. Mosquitoes buzzed around our heads as we hiked.

At last, the waterfall was visible — a shimmering cascade tumbling down a granite cliff into a deep green pool. Even from where we stood, spray, carried on the breeze, misted our faces. Nobody spoke as we stopped to take in the view.

At the base of the falls a sandy beach lay bordered by a grassy meadow. We weren't the only people who'd decided to spend the day at these falls. A few other women in various stages of undress were already tanning themselves on the sand.

"Over here," Reeva said, heading for a spot away from the water's spray.

We spread our blankets on a grassy knoll and began unpacking our knapsacks. I produced my paper bag full of cheeseballs and Allison handed me a plastic cup filled with red wine. "What's in these?" she asked, biting into one of the golden rounds, her face showing both surprise and pleasure.

"Just about everything I could find in my kitchen," I admitted. "Think of it as an adventure. You don't know what you're getting until you sink your teeth into it."

Allison gave me a long, appraising look that for some reason made me blush.

"To friends, new and old," she said, clicking my cup with hers. Others joined the toast, and I noticed Sabrina glaring at me.

Soon conversation was flowing easily, and for once the women refrained from their habitual bickering. Holly was giving Fay a run for her money in the cool and aloof department, watching everyone else with a half-smile. Billie was trying to get Karen interested in the woman she'd brought along, but Karen seemed intent on trying to jolly Sabrina out of her pouting. Reeva was clearly smitten with her new, navel-ringed girlfriend, and the usually loquacious Lacy was busy eating everything in sight. Allison sat down next to me and did her best to be flirtatious. I lost count of the number of times her hand brushed mine or rested against my leg. For my part, it was fairly easy to reciprocate. Allison was hard to ignore.

After lunch, Karen organized a football game. As much as I enjoyed the sport, this time I was looking forward to watching the way the women played — not just because of the football references in the notes, but because I'd learned years ago, before I'd ever thought of becoming a P.I., that you can learn a lot about a person by the way they handle winning and losing. I was curious to see them interact on the field.

"Losers have to tote all the trash back," Karen said. "Come on, let's choose sides. Reeva, you be the other captain."

Reeva pulled herself away from her new friend and palmed the football. "I'll take Fay," she said. Fay looked surprised, but went to stand beside her. Reeva probably thought that with Fay's sturdy body, she'd make a good blocker.

"I'll take the cowgirl," Karen said. I was starting to dislike the nickname, but I walked over and stood by her anyway.

Karen and Reeva quickly chose their teams and called us into their huddles. Karen began barking out her orders like a seasoned drill sergeant and Allison, who was on our team, elbowed me in the ribs.

"Just humor them, okay? Karen lives for these games almost as much as Reeva."

As the game got underway, I marveled at the marked difference in the way the two women quarterbacked their teams. Karen marched us down the field in an orderly if boring fashion. She handed off to me or Peaches, tossed little swing passes to Sabrina and called a ridiculous number of quarterback sneaks. She virtually ignored Allison, who ran the deep patterns, and it finally occurred to me that Karen didn't have much of an arm.

Reeva had a cannon. She handed off to Lacy just often enough to mix things up, but relied heavily on Billie's ability to snatch the ball out of the air on a dead run. Just as often, Reeva threw to Holly who, without seeming to break a sweat, managed to be in the right place at the right time. Sure enough, Fay was used primarily as a blocker, which didn't seem to thrill her in the least.

Even with Reeva's superior arm, we managed to stay close, in part due to Sabrina's diligence in pursuing the ball carrier, and in part due to Karen's ball-control tactics. It took them a couple of plays to score. It took us an eternity.

"Isn't it about time for a beer break?" Lacy

asked, gasping for air. She wasn't the only one ready for a breather. We'd been at it for over an hour.

"Score's tied." Reeva looked a little winded herself. "Let's go one more. First team to score, wins it." She flipped a coin and Karen called heads. Grumbling, Reeva tossed Karen the ball.

"Maybe we should mix it up," Allison said in the huddle. "Let's take one deep." It was the first time she'd come close to complaining about the fact that Karen hadn't thrown to her. She'd run a country mile and hadn't yet touched the ball.

"We can't risk the interception. Billie's too fast."

With that, Karen called a series of the same predictable plays she'd called all afternoon. Naturally, the other side seemed to anticipate each call. After three downs, Karen had been sacked once, thrown a short completion to Sabrina that netted almost no yards, and tried a quarterback sneak that gained only a couple. We were facing fourth and long and Reeva was chomping at the bit.

"Let's go for it," Sabrina said.

"On fourth down?" Karen was incredulous. "You know it's not a high percentage play. If we don't make it, we're just handing them the game."

"I can make it," Allison said. "Just throw long."

"That's exactly what they'll be expecting," Karen said.

"Not if I'm the one to throw it," I spoke up. They all looked at me. "Set it up like you're going to go short to Sabrina. When Reeva rushes you, toss the ball back to me. I'll throw long to Allison."

It said something about Karen that as much as she hated relinquishing control of the football, her resolve to win was stronger. Even so, I wasn't sure she would actually do it, but at the last second, with Reeva bearing down on her, Karen flipped me the ball.

I pump-faked to Sabrina, which drew Billie off Allison for just a moment. It wasn't much, but Allison took advantage of the brief separation and broke for the end zone. Sending a quick prayer skyward, I reached back and gave it everything I had. The ball sailed through the air, an imperfect spiral, rocketing toward Allison's outstretched hands. I saw her leap, like a graceful gazelle fully extended, her hands almost touching the ball. Then, without any sense that it was coming, something huge and devastating slammed into me, knocking me to the ground.

I've been knocked out before, but never without a moment's warning. This time there was no chance to brace myself for the impact. When I opened my eyes, Reeva was standing over me, red-faced, a look of absolute shame in her eyes. The other faces were hazy and out of focus.

"You're bleeding," Lacy said, touching my lip with a tissue from her pocket. "I thought this was supposed to be touch football," she spat at Reeva.

"I couldn't pull up," Reeva said. "I was going for the ball. I didn't mean to hit her."

"Shit, Reeva. The ball was already in the end zone when you decked her," Allison said, panting. She still had the ball in her hands, and despite her concern, she looked absolutely radiant. She'd finally gotten to catch the ball.

"Nice catch," I said. I forced myself to sit up, feeling suddenly queasy. There was a good amount of blood splattered on the front of my shirt, and I could tell my lower lip was already twice its usual size.

"Hey, look. I'm sorry, okay?" Reeva looked as miserable as anyone I'd ever seen. Even Fay had given her a disapproving scowl.

"It's okay," I said. "No hard feelings." Billie came running up with a cold beer, and pressed it against my lip. When I winced, she pulled it back. "Just open it, okay?" She did, and I took a tentative sip out of one side of my mouth, then held the cold can gingerly against my lip. Allison held her hand out to me, helping me up.

"Nice throw," Karen said as we walked back toward the blankets. Somehow, she didn't seem that happy about it, though. Moments earlier, it seemed she'd have done anything to win. Now that she had, she wasn't all that ecstatic.

"It was pure luck. I just closed my eyes and heaved it. Allison did all the work."

Allison, who still hadn't let go of the ball, was beaming. "Come on, let's go for a swim," she said.

"I think I'll sit this one out." My lip was throbbing and I really did have a headache.

"You need someone to stay with you?" Billie asked.

"No, really. But thanks. I'll be fine."

I watched them peel off their clothes, some wearing bathing suits, others not, and hike down to the base of the falls. The afternoon sun was still quite warm, and while the idea of a dip in the water was appealing, it was nice just lying where I was, babying myself. Before I knew it, I dozed off.

The bad thing was down there all right. I could

see its evil eyes gleaming beneath the water. It was searching through the darkness for me, and I tried not to move, lest it find me. But I needed air. As stealthily as I could, I propelled myself toward the surface. I'd almost made it when the thing's grip seized my ankle, yanking me downward. My lungs were bursting, but instead of fighting against it, I turned and dove straight for it. Its head was covered with something dark, but the eyes looked vaguely familiar. I was almost close enough to grab whatever was covering its head, when it abruptly let go of my ankle and disappeared into the depths below. With one last burst of energy, I shot forward and gulped the fresh air into my lungs.

"Hey, girlfriend. You okay?" Billie's kind eyes were the first thing I saw upon waking. My heart was pounding.

"Just a dream I keep having," I said. "I'm afraid it's trying to tell me something. Like a premonition. Where's Allison?" I couldn't shake the feeling that the dream was trying to warn me of some imminent danger.

"They decided to hike up to the top. Me, I've had enough exercise for one day. If I'd have had to run downfield one more time, I'd have keeled over."

"The top of the waterfall? Did everyone go?" I was trying not to sound panicked, but my voice was giving me away.

"Well, Allison went first. Sabrina followed after her and Karen and Fay took off after Sabrina. I think Reeva and Harriet went into the woods to mess around. I'm not sure who else was going. I decided to come get something cold to drink. Why? What's wrong?"

"Come on," I said, getting to my feet.

"Cassidy, what's the matter? You're freaking me out."

"I'll tell you later. I promise. Right now, I just want to find Allison." I started jogging toward the base of the waterfall, Billie right beside me.

"Does this have something to do with that dream you were having?"

"I hope not." The truth was, I didn't know.

Chapter Eleven

There were several trails leading to the top of the waterfall and I had no idea which one Allison had taken. The path we chose was rocky and slippery with moss but looked like the most direct route. There were dozens of side trails leading off into the woods, and every time we passed one, I wondered if Allison had wandered off to pick flowers or had gone straight up to the top. I had nothing to go on but my instincts, which I knew from experience were sometimes eerily accurate, sometimes sadistically false.

We were about halfway to the top when we

rounded a bend and ran into Reeva's friend, Harriet, bent over a patch of mushrooms next to the trail.

"Look what I found!" she said. "These morels cost over twelve dollars a pound in the store, and that's if you can even find them! They're all over the place up here." She'd collected quite a pile of them and made a make-shift basket out of Reeva's flannel shirt. I picked up one of the mushrooms and examined the reddish-brown, brain-like folds of the cap. I dropped the mushroom on the ground and wiped my hands on my pants.

"You haven't eaten any?" I said. Harriet looked at me, her almond eyes suddenly huge.

"No. Why?"

"These aren't morels," I said. "They're called false morels, also known as turban fungus. If you eat them raw, they're deadly. You should wash your hands."

Harriet threw the shirt to the ground and backed up, clearly terrified.

"Where's Reeva?" I asked.

"She went on up to the top of the waterfall. I told her I'd meet her there after I finished picking these. You're positive they're poisonous?" She was scrubbing her hands against her bicycle shorts frantically.

"I took a class," I explained. "There are so many wild mushrooms growing where I live, I wanted to be sure." I was already moving up the trail as I spoke. Billie was right behind me.

"Maybe that's what your dream was trying to tell you," she said. "If you hadn't come along, she might have eaten one."

"Maybe," I said. But if so, why did I still feel such an urgent sense of dread?

The waterfall cascaded down the rocky face of the cliff to our left and we could see the top every now and then through the trees. We were almost there, when the path turned and we suddenly had a clear view of the ridge. There, standing over the falls like a red-headed angel with wings spread, was Allison, exulting in the view. Billie and I stopped. She was alone, and apparently quite safe. My hammering heart slowed to a mere thud.

"Did I mention that most of my premonitions are false alarms?" I said, grinning at Billie.

"Actually, you failed to mention that. Come on, we may as well go on up. We're almost there anyway."

We were about to continue, when suddenly something small and round like a rock came hurtling out of the woods toward the bluff, striking Allison on the back of the head. She fell forward, knees landing on the edge of the cliff. From where we were, we could barely see her. Then, before either of us could move, another rock followed the first.

Billie and I raced up the path, scrambling on all fours at times, scraping our knees and knuckles as we forced ourselves up the rocky trail. When we reached the top, we looked around frantically. Allison was nowhere in sight.

I ran to the spot where I thought she'd been standing and forced myself to look down. There, a few feet below the top of the cliff was a short ledge. Allison's body dangled in the air above the raging falls, one foot wedged into a tentative foothold. Her fingers dug into the rock of the ledge below us.

"Allison!" I yelled above the roar of the waterfall. "Hold on!" My heart was in my throat and my ears were pounding.

"What are we going to do?" Billie shrieked. Her eyes were wide, and I knew she was as terrified as I was.

"Do you have a belt?" She shook her head and we both glanced around frantically for something Allison could hang on to. There was nothing but rock and plants.

"If you can hold onto my ankles, I think I can get down far enough to get hold of her wrists and pull her up. When I do, you'll need to pull me back up by my ankles."

"Pull you both up? I don't know if I can, Cassidy." I didn't know either, but I didn't see any alternative. Allison wouldn't be able to hold on much longer. I lay on the ground and inched forward, my head suspended above the hundred-foot drop. I felt Billie's fingernails dig into my ankle and welcomed the pain. As long as she didn't let go, I didn't care how deeply she dug.

"I'll have to go lower!" I shouted. "You need to ease up some!"

Billie was pulling back so hard, I wasn't able to reach Allison's wrists. I could see Allison's face, pressed against the granite wall, her eyes closed. Her hair was plastered against her scalp with sweat, and blood was trickling from her ear. Her knuckles were white and I feared her grip was fading fast. She still had a toe-hold, but if her hands slipped, it wouldn't be enough to hold her.

Billie inched forward, easing me down another half-foot. The blood pumped in my head, and I knew my face was beet red.

"A little more, Billie. Come on!" I felt her nails dig into bone as she held onto my ankles, moving closer to the cliff edge. At last I was able to reach Allison's wrists. They were slick with sweat as I tried to get a good grip.

"Hold on a little longer, Allie!"

Even though I was right above her, I had to shout over the roar of the waterfall. I wiped my hands on my shirt, trying to dry them, and grabbed her wrists again. If my hands slipped, well, I couldn't allow myself to think about that possibility.

"You can let go of the rock, Allison! Just let go and grab onto my wrists!"

Slowly, she turned her head upward and for the first time, she opened her eyes. I tried to appear calm, but with all the blood having rushed to my head, I'm not sure I pulled it off. My eyes were already starting to bulge.

"Grab my wrists!" I commanded.

Her eyes locked with mine and, after what seemed an eternity, she let go with first one hand and then the other, digging her fingers into the flesh of my wrists. The sudden weight of her body tugged me downward.

"Now, Billie! Pull us up!"

My arms ached and trembled as I tried to pull Allison upward while Billie struggled to pull my legs back up the cliff. It was like being pulled apart. I could feel the muscles in my thighs stretching and my shoulders felt as though they were being ripped from their sockets.

I willed myself to ignore the pain and thought of all those stories in which people suddenly have super-human strength and are able to lift the car that's just fallen on someone. No sooner had I thought it, than Billie seemed to be endowed with that super-human strength herself. With a sudden burst, Allison and I were miraculously hauled up the side of the cliff and onto the safety of the ridge.

When I dared to open my eyes, I was surprised to see Reeva and Sabrina standing over us. Billie was sprawled on the ground beside me. It had been Reeva who'd added the extra strength Billie needed to haul us up.

"What happened?" Sabrina asked, kneeling over Allison.

"I slipped," Allison said. "I got too close to the edge." Billie and I exchanged glances, and when she opened her mouth, I shook my head. She narrowed her eyes, but kept quiet.

"You're bleeding!" Sabrina said, noticing the red, sticky mass in Allison's hair. I noticed Allison's fingernails were bloody as well.

"You shouldn't have come up here alone," Reeva said.

"I thought you guys were right behind me." Allison looked pointedly at Sabrina.

"I had to pee," she said, looking mortified. "I had trouble finding the path again."

"There *is* more than one way up here," Reeva said in her defense. "I saw Karen take off on a path halfway back and she's still not here. I left Harriet picking mushrooms somewhere."

"They were poisonous," Billie said. When everyone looked at her, she explained.

"Hey, what's going on?" Karen said, coming up the path, clearly winded.

"Allison almost killed herself falling down the cliff," Reeva said. "We had to pull her back up."

Karen glanced at Sabrina who was holding her

shirttail to Allison's scalp, trying to stop the bleeding. Then she looked at me. "If she's the one who fell off the cliff, how come Billie and the cowgirl are the ones who look so exhausted?"

Nobody felt like explaining.

"I better go check on Harriet," Reeva said. "Jesus, what a day!"

"You okay to walk?" I asked Allison.

"I'll help her down," Sabrina said. She was hovering over Allison like a mother hen.

Karen shot her a pained look but didn't say anything. Slowly, Billie and I got to our feet. "Why don't you guys go first," I said to Sabrina. "We'll be right behind you."

"I wouldn't want to slow you down," she said. "I mean, Allison might want to take it a little slower. Why don't you all just go on ahead."

"Oh, for God's sake," Allison said, getting to her feet. "I'll go first. You can all follow me." Sabrina looked hurt, which seemed to make Karen angry. I looked at Billie and shrugged. There were more emotions flying around this group than I'd ever be able to sort out. But one thing I did know for sure, someone really did want Allison out of the picture, and they'd almost succeeded. Whoever it was, she was getting pretty bold. At least now I knew for sure it wasn't Billie.

As she and I slowly brought up the rear, I worked the kinks out of my muscles and wondered where Holly, Fay and Lacy were. Still wandering along one of the paths, trying to find their way to the top of the waterfall? Or was one of them lurking in the woods, watching our descent, cursing their foiled attempt?

Chapter Twelve

Dinner was strained, and for reasons I couldn't untangle, there seemed to be a great deal of tension at the table. Lacy was her usual perky self, doting on Allison, which seemed to infuriate Sabrina, who hadn't let Allison out of her sight since our return from the falls. I'd seen what I thought was the full array of Sabrina's mood swings, but tonight she seemed downright spooky. She kept gracing me with long, wounded looks, and then would turn her attention back to Allison, watching her with adoration one minute, pouting the next. Karen stormed away from the table before she'd even finished eating, and Reeva seemed irked beyond reason. It wasn't until I saw her new girlfriend, Harriet, head toward the dance floor with another woman, that I realized Reeva had been dumped.

Holly was watching the whole scene with her usual detached amusement. I wondered what it would take to rattle her cage. I just don't trust people who are that cool all the time. It makes me think they're hiding something. I also wondered where Fay was. She hadn't joined us for dinner.

"Girlfriend, we've got to talk," Billie whispered. She was looking damn sexy, I thought. Her dark skin was set off by a white caftan, and she wore bright red beads for accent. She'd even adorned her close-cropped hair with a red begonia she'd picked in the woods. Allison was watching us with curiosity.

I nodded at Billie, but before I could answer, Allison nudged me under the table with her toe. "Let's dance," she said, smiling seductively.

I sighed and shrugged. "Later," I said to Billie, then followed Allison to the dance floor.

"I'm scared," she said, sliding into my arms. We'd hardly had a chance to talk since we'd been back. Sabrina had insisted on accompanying Allison to the cabin, and I'd had to crouch in the closet to watch them through the camera lens, just to make sure Allison was safe.

"Me too," I admitted. It was a nice, slow song, and we moved easily together. "I'm going to tell Billie. It can't hurt to have another set of eyes. Our stalker is getting reckless. Besides, Billie saw the rocks."

"If you hadn't done what you did —"

114

"Shhh . . ." I felt her move closer, burying her face against my neck. She wasn't playacting. I could feel her body tremble.

"I owe you my life."

"Allie, don't. When it's all over, I'll let you buy me a really nice bottle of wine. Besides, you're paying me, remember? In the meantime, let's just stay focused on finding the damn stalker." I felt her let out her breath. It was warm and moist against my neck.

"Do you have any ideas?"

"Too many," I said truthfully. "I think Sabrina's so full of love and hate for you she doesn't know which end is up. And she may be suicidal — there's a touch of Sylvia Plath in her poetry — and sometimes suicidal people turn homicidal too." I took a breath. "I think Reeva just plain hates you, out of sheer envy, and after what she did to me today, I see she's got a violent streak. Besides, her obsession with football does coincide nicely with the notes. On the other hand, she did help Billie pull us up."

"So did Sabrina," Allison pointed out.

"I guess neither one of them could very well refuse, with the other one there."

"What about Karen?"

"You know that picture you showed me of the whole group in the snow? She's got a copy of that in her wallet, except you've been cut out of it."

Allison was silent, taking this in. Suddenly she laughed.

"What?" I asked. Her breath was tickling my skin, raising goosebumps all the way down my arm.

"In that picture, I've got my arm around Sabrina, right?"

"So?"

"So, Karen's madly in love with Sabrina. Haven't you noticed? She was furious when we started dating. It was right around the time that picture was taken."

Suddenly, I understood all those looks I'd seen Karen giving Sabrina every time Sabrina fawned over Allison. And I understood why Sabrina had been Karen's favorite receiver this afternoon. I'd thought it was because Karen doubted her own throwing skills. But it was just as possible, I realized, that she'd been showing unabashed favoritism.

"That gives her a motive," I said. "She hates you because Sabrina prefers you to her."

The song ended, and another one started. Allison tightened her arms around me and we continued dancing.

"Anyone else?" she asked.

"Lacy seems normal enough. I just can't figure out why she'd hide her Bible."

"What?"

I explained how I'd found Lacy's Bible in her pillowcase when I'd searched her room.

"I didn't even know she was religious," Allison said. "Not that anyone would care. Lately, I've been feeling pretty damned religious myself."

"Frankly, Holly and Fay remain a mystery. I didn't get a chance to search Holly's cabin, but she's about the most aloof person I've ever met. Always has that smug smile on her lips, like she knows a secret. And she acts so superior to everyone else. That she probably knows you've willed two million dollars to Women On Top, and the fact that she'll be in charge of those funds once you die, gives her a pretty damned good motive. As for Fay, she's either the shyest woman on earth or she's hiding something. I get the feeling she's constantly biting her tongue, dying to say something, but holding back. Maybe I just don't trust people who reveal so little of themselves. They both make me nervous."

"I had no idea you were such a cynic." She sighed against my neck, sending another flurry of goosebumps down my body. I pulled away. "Your lip looks terrible," she said, touching it with her fingertip. It was puffy and sore. Dinner had been tricky.

"I guess Reeva really wanted to win," I said.

Allison leaned forward and kissed me lightly on the lips.

"Hey," I said, stepping farther away.

"Hey, yourself. You're supposed to be my girl-friend. Besides, you saved my life today. It wouldn't be natural not to show my appreciation."

She leaned forward again and pressed her lips to mine, gently insistent. Despite the tenderness of my lips, despite the warnings in my head, my lips responded, sending ripples of pleasure through the rest of my body.

"Allie, don't." I pulled away abruptly, holding her at arm's length.

"That's okay," she said. "On that one kiss, I'll get through the rest of this evening."

We danced until the song ended, holding each other at a safe distance, yet I was intensely aware of her body inches from my own. When the song was over, I nearly bolted for the door.

"I need to address the new arrivals anyway," she said, smiling. "But don't go too far. I may need you."

On my way back to the table, I literally ran into Karen. As she had the night before, she was wearing all black.

"Hey, cowgirl. I see you haven't been bucked off yet." She grinned lewdly, and her eyes looked slightly glazed over from alcohol.

"I beg your pardon?" I felt my cheeks growing warm.

"I admire a woman who can stay in the saddle with Allison. She's as wild a ride as they come." When I didn't laugh, she went on. "Why, I remember not being able to walk for a week. But then, you two haven't had that much time alone yet. You'll see what I mean."

I felt my hands bunch into fists at my side.

"There a problem here?" Reeva said, stepping up behind me. She must have noticed my stance.

"Nah, I was just telling the cowgirl what kind of ride she could expect tonight."

"And I was just getting ready to explain to Karen that where I come from, women don't talk in derogatory terms about ex-lovers and friends."

"Shit, where the fuck is that? Walton's mountain?" Reeva's face was flushed and her words were somewhat slurred. Like Karen, she'd been drinking since we'd come back from the falls.

Karen guffawed. "That's good, Reeva. Damn, all this time I've been calling her cowgirl, but she's really John Girl, John Boy's long lost sister on Walton's Mountain."

I smiled, letting my fists relax. "That would be

funny, wouldn't it? I mean it would make a pretty good movie."

"What's that?" Reeva asked.

"*You* know. John Girl meets Beavis and Butt-head." I smiled sweetly and headed for the door, half afraid they'd follow me outside, half hoping they would.

Chapter Thirteen

"Damn, girl. I thought I was gonna have to come to your defense there." Billie's hand on my shoulder made me start, but it was oddly comforting.

"Come on," I said. "Let's get out of here before they come looking for me." We headed down toward the lake.

"Beavis and Butt-head?" she asked, linking her bracelet-laden arm through mine. We jangled as we walked. "Honey, that was sweet. The best part was when you walked out. Reeva turned to Karen and said, 'Which one of us do you figure she just called a butthead?' I nearly choked on my wine!"

"Someone's trying to kill Allison," I blurted.

Billie stopped in her tracks and turned to face me. Her dark eyes burned with intensity. "So I noticed. You wanna tell me what's going on, or am I supposed to guess?"

I told her. We walked down to the lakeshore and sat on one of the wooden benches, looking across at the island. The moon was nearly full, its light licking the water like flames. When I'd finished, Billie reached out and held my hand.

"I should've known something was up. Damn, why didn't she tell me?"

"How could she tell anyone? She doesn't know who's trying to kill her. All she knows is that it's someone in your group. In fact, you're the only one we've ruled out."

"I can't believe this." Billie got up and began to pace in front of the bench. She'd taken the flower from her hair and was twirling it between her fingers. "I'll tell you what," she said. "I don't think it's Reeva. I mean, the first down, second down thing fits, but I don't know. She's too literal, you know? I mean, throwing the rock might be Reeva's style, but not the bees. Not the poisoned cereal. Sure, she could've done the brake lines, but I don't think she would have. For one thing, that kind of points to her, being a mechanic and all. And second, she's more the type that would come after you with a knife."

I thought about the Swiss Army knife I'd found in her cabin and nodded. Billie was right, but Reeva simply might be smart enough to throw us all off. "So who?" I asked, standing up to pace beside her.

"I don't know. Damn, I wish I did. You say Holly knows about this money? Even if she does, I mean, how could that help her? It's not like she could steal it. Could she?"

"Once the money is willed to Women On Top, she could certainly control it. She's smart enough to figure out some way to get her hands on it."

"It's gotta be someone else," Billie said, shaking her head.

"Well, there's an awful lot of love/hate stuff going on around Allison," I said. "People seem to either idolize her or resent her. Has it always been this way?"

Billie laughed. "Now that I realize you two are just faking this little relationship, I can understand the question. If it were real, you wouldn't be asking."

"What do you mean?"

"I mean, anyone who's been with Allison would understand." She walked toward the water, looked up at the moon. "Allison's a special lady. She has a gift. I don't just mean that she's great with her patients, or a natural leader. Her real gift is so special, she only gives it now and then. If and when you're ever lucky enough to be on the receiving end, you'll know what I mean."

"Billie, no offense intended, but how good can someone be? I mean, I understand great sex, but come on."

Billie turned and looked at me. Her eyes were laughing and she was shaking her head. "Cassidy, listen to me, girl. It's not about sex. Not totally. When Allison's with you, she gives one thousand percent. She makes you feel like you're the most important person in the world. The *only* person in the world. Being with her is like being in a dream you don't want to wake up from." She sighed. "Picture this. A piece of chocolate that's so good, so rich, so extraordinary, when you bite into it, you swear you've found heaven. Best thing you've ever tasted. One piece is almost more than you can bear. You'd like more, but you know instinctively that it wouldn't be good for you. It would be too much of a good thing. Now, here's Allison, and she's got a whole box of these chocolates. There's no way one person can handle the whole thing. And what's she gonna do? Let it rot? She knows what she's got. She appreciates it as much as the people she shares the gift with. She offers them sparingly, when the time is right."

"You make her sound like some kind of sex goddess," I said.

"Do I?" She looked wistful, then sighed. "It's not so much the sex as it is the intensity. It's — Oh hell, Cass. Some things are better left unexplained."

We'd started walking along the shore, and I was glad Billie couldn't see my face. "You're saying that her gift is her love, but it's so wonderful that the average person just can't handle it? I'm supposed to believe that all these women she goes to bed with are just grateful for the opportunity to be her latest conquest? I should introduce her to Erica Trinidad."

Billie laughed. "I don't know who she is, but this Erica sounds interesting."

I chose to say nothing.

"Look, Cassidy. I'm only telling you this because of what's happening. You think someone's trying to kill Allison out of jealousy, but I'm not sure that's right. I can only speak for myself, of course. I mean, I can imagine someone wanting to be with her again, but no one in her right mind would think they could possibly handle Allison full-time. She's just too intense."

We had walked all the way to a small pier where dozens of tiny sailboats were moored. We turned back. I was as intrigued with the conversation as I was disturbed by it.

"Are you telling me that after treating these women like they're goddesses, she just drops them and they're okay with it? I don't think Sabrina is."

"I said anyone in her right mind. Sabrina's a whole different story."

"How about you? You seem to be handling Allison's infidelities just fine."

"That's just it. They're not infidelities. She's never promised herself to anyone. She's totally honest about what she can give. You feel like a damn fool accepting the conditions, but before it's over, you realize you'd have been a worse fool not to have taken advantage of the opportunity. You see? *She's* not taking advantage. *You* are. Well, not you. I mean, the women in Allison's life. I guess I mean me." She laughed at her own admission.

"So you don't feel any jealousy?" I thought I knew the answer.

She sighed heavily. "Cassidy, if Allison crept into my bed tonight, I would not turn her away. I'd welcome her with open arms. I've never loved anyone like I love Allison Crane. Not just because she's beautiful or powerful. And not just because she taught me more about myself than I imagined. I love Allison because she's a free, delicate spirit. Like a butterfly. You might want to own her, but that would mean killing her first. Those guys who chase butterflies with nets and then trap them in amber paperweights, they profess to love butterflies. But a butterfly in a paperweight is no more beautiful than a squashed bug. I think Allison counts on her lovers to accept this."

"I think one of them may have missed this point," I mused. We were almost back to the lodge and we'd both started walking more slowly.

"You like her, don't you?" she asked.

"Of course I do." It sounded pathetic, even to me.

"I mean, if you weren't on a case, you'd be interested."

"Interested or not, it wouldn't matter. I have a lover."

"But you are. Interested, I mean."

"Billie." She stopped and we stood looking at each other in the moonlight. "Allison Crane is one of the most intriguing women I've ever met, but Maggie Carradine is my lover. She's smart, she's sexy, and if I don't screw things up, I think she might just love me forever. If she ever even thought I was looking at someone else, she'd bolt. I don't want her to bolt. I have found a woman I want to spend the rest of my life with. I don't need Allison Crane." My face was hot again, and I was afraid that in the moonlight Billie could see my emotion.

"I think what I'm hearing," she said, suppressing a smile, "is that you not only love your partner, but you're trying as diligently as humanly possible to remain faithful, despite your obvious attraction to

Allison. All I can say is, good luck." She was grinning now, but her eyes were ultimately kind. "It's a noble effort, I'll give you that," she added.

I wasn't sure about the noble part, but I had to admit it was becoming something of an effort.

Allison was standing out on the lodge porch leaning against the railing. "I thought I'd been abandoned," she said. "You two out there necking without me?"

"Something like that," Billie said. "Were your ears burning?"

"Everything's burning." Her smile was seductive. She leaned closer to Billie and whispered, "Did she tell you?" Billie nodded.

"If it's all the same to you two, I'd like to turn in," I said. The truth was, I felt inordinately tired. My limbs had been stretched to the breaking point, my ankles and wrists both were gouged, my lip was throbbing and my thighs were still sore from riding Diablo. But none of that compared to the turmoil in my mind. I needed to think, and I sure as hell couldn't do that while dancing cheek to cheek with Allison Crane. Just thinking about it caused my stomach to do a ridiculous somersault which infuriated me.

Billie insisted on walking us back to our cabin, claiming it was too nice of a night to be cooped up inside. Once we were away from the lodge, she spoke up. "Why didn't you tell me!" she said, punching Allison on the arm. Then she put her arm around her and held her close.

I made Billie and Allison wait outside while I checked Allison's room. I didn't even have to go inside to know the stalker had paid a visit. On her porch, right where the welcome mat should have been, was a message spelled out in pine needles. Someone had taken a lot of time collecting the needles and arranging them just right. Someone was enjoying this little game. Allison and Billie stood beside me and we all three stared at the message: INTERFERENCE PENALTY. REPLAY THE DOWN!

Chapter Fourteen

Wednesday morning was overcast, with clouds drifting in from the west. It was cooler, too, and I pulled on a sweatshirt before heading out to the corrals in search of Buddy. Allison was sleeping soundly when I left, which didn't surprise me. She and Billie had stayed up half the night, sipping wine and giggling like schoolgirls. Even when I'd finally fallen asleep, their laughter found its way into my dreams, and for the first time in quite a while, I did not dream of the evil thing beneath the water.

Maybe Billie was right — maybe the premonition had been about Allison falling down the cliff. But with the note on the porch, that wasn't too likely. Still, the dream had left me alone last night, so maybe the worst was over.

Buddy was tethering a string of mules to a fence post when I found him. "I got your fax," he said, digging in his pocket for the folded sheets. "I thought you was in a hurry for it."

"I was. I am. Thank you." With everything that had happened yesterday, I'd forgotten about the fax until this morning. I tried to tip Buddy with a five-dollar bill, but he waved it off.

"Nah, that's okay. Say, there some kinda trouble up here? I couldn't help notice the return fax come from the police. That's why I didn't just leave it inside. I mean, I wasn't tryin' to read it or nothin', seein' as it says confidential on it but, well, it was just sort of sittin' there."

"Tell you what, Buddy. If you promise not to mention this fax, or anything you might've read to anyone, just for a few days, I promise to tell you the whole story just as soon as I can. Deal?"

"Deal," he said.

Just what I needed, I thought. Now I had to worry about Buddy blowing my cover. I walked down toward the lake and sat on a boulder where no one passing by could look over my shoulder. One glance at the pages told me Martha had outdone herself.

This will cost you, Cass. I'm thinking chocolate mousse with raspberry sauce at the very least, and a very good Cabernet. Just for starters.

One of your pals has a record. Lacy Watkins was arrested in 1989 for disturbing the peace. She was harassing women trying to get into an abortion clinic. Pretty weird, if you ask me, for someone working for WOT. Her father was a minister for a church called Holy Savior, active in the pro-life movement, so that's probably the connection.

Other points of interest: Karen Castillo got herself a dishonorable discharge from the Navy. With time, we could probably find out why. It could be nothing more than getting caught in some recruit's bed, but you never know. And speaking of the military, Fay Daniels checked out of the Army less than a year ago, after being in since high school. And get this — she's married. Who knows? Maybe she just recently came out.

And just fyi, the lovely Ms. Crane is loaded. Could be relevant.

Also, Reeva Dunsmore once threatened someone with a knife. Turned out to be a lovers' dispute. The woman didn't press charges. The police were called out, so they logged the call and her name came up on the computer. This was three years ago.

Hope you're taking care of yourself. Sounds like you're surrounded by real interesting characters. Ha! Maggie's beside herself with jealousy, especially when I let it slip that you were posing as Allison's girlfriend. I can't believe you didn't tell her that part! Way to

go, Cass. I think I smoothed it over, though.
Sort of.

Hugs and Kisses,
Martha.

Damn, I thought, walking back to the cabin. Now
I had to worry about Maggie on top of everything
else. The most intriguing information was that little
Lacy Watkins, who hid her Bible under her pillow,
had once been arrested for blockading an abortion
clinic. What she was doing working for a lesbian
organization like Women On Top was beyond me.
Unless she was some kind of religious right-wing
fanatic working undercover. But why?

It's true, Allison's first thought when she found
the bees in her office was that the attack had been
political. But what would anyone hope to accomplish
by killing Allison? Someone else would just step
forward and take her place as president. Women On
Top would survive, and considering Allison's inheritance, the organization would be, at least financially,
better off. It just didn't make sense to kill one
person when they could just as easily bomb the whole
group, building and all. And it was becoming increasingly clear that the attacks on Allison were
personal in nature.

But were they really trying to kill her? So far, the
only thing all the attacks had in common, aside from
the football references, was that they were surprisingly unsuccessful. I was pretty sure that if I had
wanted to kill someone, I'd have accomplished the
task by now. There were plenty of ways to commit

murder. It seemed to me that all of the attempts so far had been pretty much hit or miss. Maybe whoever was doing this, was more interested in scaring Allison than in actually killing her.

On the other hand, had the bees actually attacked, had she eaten her cereal or her pâté, had the cars not swerved out of the way when her brakes had been cut, or had Billie and I not come along when we did, it was quite possible that Allison would be dead by now. Or, at the very least, badly hurt.

And why the notes in the first place? Obviously, the attacker was into games, and not just football. Perhaps the real motive wasn't murder so much as terror. If that were true, this person was achieving more success than I was giving her credit for. I shook my head and tried to focus on Martha's notes.

I wondered about Karen's dishonorable discharge. It didn't surprise me that she'd been in the military. No civilian made beds that neatly. I'd been right about Fay, too. She *had* been in the Army and she had been married. That she still was, puzzled me. What was a married woman doing with WOT? I thought about Reeva's comment that half the dykes she knew were married and wondered if she'd been thinking of Fay. Could it be that Fay was just testing the waters? What I'd taken for shyness might have been ambiguity about her own sexuality.

What didn't surprise me in the least was that Reeva had once attacked someone with a knife. I had a puffed lip attesting to the fact that she had trouble controlling her temper, and I'd already found a knife in her cabin. The more I learned about Reeva, the less I liked her.

Smoke rose in a lazy swirl from Allison's chimney,

so I knew she was up. I could smell coffee and cinnamon rolls when I entered my cabin and my stomach rumbled appreciatively. I tapped on the bathroom door.

"It's open," she called. She was wearing turquoise sweats that matched her eyes and complemented her fair complexion. Her reddish gold hair was tousled and I realized with a start that she was, as Billie said, a strikingly beautiful woman. I forced the thought from my head. "Coffee?" she asked, handing me a cup.

"Thanks. Allie, did you know Karen Castillo had a dishonorable discharge from the Navy?"

"Oh, sure. She told me herself. She said it was a bogus charge. Supposedly, she decked an officer, but she says it was really just a lovers' quarrel that got out of hand. When the woman got physical with her, Karen slapped her. Unfortunately, another officer witnessed the slap and reported it. The lover, afraid that the truth would result in her own discharge, said Karen had been insubordinate."

"Did you know Lacy Watkins was arrested once for protesting at an abortion clinic? And that her father is a minister with ties to anti-choice groups?"

"Jesus, Cass, where are you getting all this?"

I told her about Martha's fax.

"Like I told you yesterday, I didn't even know Lacy was religious. And I don't care. Some of my best friends are religious." She smiled and I helped myself to a cinnamon roll.

"It's just a little incongruous," I said. "Not very many right-to-lifers work in lesbian political groups. How well do you know her?"

"Apparently not as well as I thought. But just

because her father's a right-wing minister doesn't mean she is. How long ago was this arrest?"

"Nineteen eighty-nine. She couldn't have been much over eighteen."

"When I was eighteen, I was engaged to a guy named Wally Walbright. People do change, Cass."

It was true. But I intended to ask Lacy about it anyway — if I could figure out a way to do it without blowing my cover.

"What time is your meeting this morning? As soon as Holly leaves, I want to get a look at her cabin. Sooner or later I've got to be able to rule someone out besides Billie."

"Ten o'clock. You're not coming?"

"No. In fact, I think I'll skip breakfast, too. As long as you stay by Billie, you should be safe. I'll just have another of your rolls," I said, helping myself.

"I hope we didn't keep you up last night." She stood with her back to the fire. "We got into reminiscing."

"Can I ask you something personal?"

"Don't be ridiculous. You saved my life yesterday. You've videotaped me naked. Of course you can ask me something personal."

I ignored the videotape remark and took a sip of my coffee. "Have you ever thought about settling down? With one person? I mean, with someone like Billie, for example. It's obvious you really care about each other, and she's incredibly attractive. I just wondered if you ever got tired of playing the field."

I expected her to laugh, or shrug it off with a witty remark, but instead she got up to pour more coffee. "Someday, maybe," she said finally. She let out a huge sigh. "I don't trust myself, I guess. It's not that I wouldn't love to have someone to share everything with, but I know I'd end up hurting them. Like before." To my astonishment, she started to cry, her eyes filling with tears which ran down her cheeks unchecked. There was no sound. Her shoulders didn't heave. She just stood there, letting the tears flow.

"I'm sorry. It's none of my business."

She cut me off. "I've never spoken of it." She paused long enough for me to think she wouldn't continue, then she drew in a deep breath and went on. "My first true love was Mary Ann." She took another deep breath, closing her eyes, remembering. "Mary Ann Anderson," she almost whispered. "I called her Andy." She slowly exhaled and looked directly me. "Andy killed herself. Back in high school. Because I dumped her. I didn't want to be gay, you see, but I was so in love with her I couldn't help myself. It was incredible. We'd sit for hours, gazing into each other's eyes, just holding hands. My body was on fire, I loved her so much. My mother caught us kissing, and she refused to let me see her anymore. When I started dating Wally, Andy begged me to stop. I told her it was over between us, that what we'd felt was wrong, and that I didn't feel that way anymore. It was a lie, but I wanted it to be true." She paused. "She hung herself with the belt from her bathrobe. Her suicide note was written to me." Allison's pale skin was blotchy with emotion as the tears slid down her face.

First Andy, I thought, and then her parents. No wonder Allison was afraid to love anyone. "You know it wasn't your fault," I offered lamely.

She shook her head emphatically. "I know it was.

I did the wrong thing. I tried to convince myself afterwards that I was in love with Wally, that I always had been. It was my way of justifying what I'd done to Andy. Poor Wally. He never stood a chance. I ended up hurting him too, of course."

"I'm not an expert, Allie, but it seems to me you stand a better chance of hurting people the way your life is now than if you settled down with just one woman. This way, you just end up breaking everyone's heart."

"But I tell them!" she yelled, making me start. She began pacing in front of the fireplace. I'd noticed the little cabin had grown quite warm.

"I never promise anybody anything. I take nothing from them. I give what I can, and then I leave them alone. I never lead anyone to believe I'm in love with them. Even if I am."

"Because you're afraid they'll love you back? And that you'll let them down? And that they might kill themselves because of it? Allison, you've got to get past it. What happened to Mary Ann was half a lifetime ago. You can't let it ruin your whole life."

"I thought you said you weren't an expert," she said. "Now all the sudden you sound like Sigmund Fucking Freud. I'm going to take a shower!"

Just like that, she was gone. I waited for the sound of the shower door closing before tiptoeing through the bathroom to my own side. I felt miserable. I'd had no right to pry, and less right to offer advice. I just couldn't believe that someone as shrewd and professional as Allison Crane could be so badly haunted by her past. Billie was wrong. Allison was no butterfly. She was still trapped in the cocoon she'd made for herself all those years ago.

Chapter Fifteen

Allison clearly didn't want to talk about it anymore, acting instead as if the conversation had never taken place. I left her at Billie's just before ten and headed over to Holly McIntyre's cabin, glad that most of the women were already at breakfast or attending one of the morning workshops.

I waited behind a cluster of trees just across from Holly's cabin, keeping an eye on the door. She seemed to have a habit of showing up late for meals, and just as I expected, it was almost ten before she emerged from her cabin. She was wearing an expensive-looking wool jacket over a silk blouse tucked into jeans and boots. As usual, she looked calm and collected, every blond strand of her Farrah Fawcett hairdo in perfect place. I watched her saunter toward the lodge, not a care in the world.

Looking around to make sure no one was watching, I made my way to her door and let myself in. Holly's cabin was tidy but not sterile like Karen's. Right away, I noticed a book on mushrooms next to the bed and thumbed through it. I had a few similar books myself, and like mine, hers had a section on the poisonous ones. I noticed a few dog-eared pages and once again wondered what exactly had been in that pâte someone had left for Allison. A few chopped mushrooms would be just as effective as rat poison, I thought, and harder to trace.

Holly's clothes were neatly hung in the closet, revealing a surprisingly expensive wardrobe. She had enough clothes for a month and most of them were in the semi-dressy mode. I found a purse hanging on a hook in the closet and looked through it. Her wallet held no pictures, just credit cards, cash, driver's license and small change. The rest of the purse was equally barren. Small brush, mirror, nothing of interest. The bureau drawers were likewise neat, orderly and mundane. I'd given up worrying about pâte, but I checked her refrigerator anyway and found nothing notable. About to conclude that Holly McIntyre was as boring as she was aloof, I thought to slide my hand under her pillow and felt the hard edges of a book.

Another secret Bible reader? I wondered. Maybe Women On Top was teeming with religious zealots. I carefully slid the book out and willed myself to breathe slowly when I saw what it was. At last, someone who really did keep a diary.

Holly's handwriting was full of loops and curves. Her journal, as she referred to it, was apparently written with the intent of being of future use if and when she decided to write her memoirs. She was extremely factual in terms of dates and times, but more salient were the comments she made after each account. They weren't just biting and sarcastic, they were mean.

5/23/95 — 3:00 PM — Reeva just called to invite me to a barbecue next Saturday. She made it clear she wasn't inviting everyone from WOT, just select members, and she wanted me to keep it quiet. Like I'd really want to go to one of her little barbecues. I can see it now. Football game blaring from the television in the living room (the fact she even has a TV in the living room should tell you something), a bunch of bulldykes swigging beer in the backyard while their femme fatale playmates ooh and ahh over them. But I told her I'd be there. A few of the women are at least interesting. They'll make great characters someday, should I decide to write about them. Of course, I could never write about Reeva. She's such a stereotype no one would find her credible.

I flipped through the pages, reading one stinging comment after another. No one was spared. Holly's colleagues at the newspaper were blasted as often as the women from WOT. She even ridiculed the women she dated, calling one a "cloying pest." I was trying to hurry but found myself riveted. When I heard footsteps on the porch, my heart nearly stopped.

There was no time to put the book back. No time to think. I dove under the bed, taking the journal with me just as I heard the key turn in the knob.

The door banged open and Holly swept into the room. I held my breath, willing my heart to quit hammering, sure she'd be able to hear it.

I could see her snakeskin boots, inches from my face. She was at the foot of the bed, apparently changing her shirt. When she flung her shirt to the floor, I saw why the sudden need for a change. Holly had spilled coffee down the front of her silk blouse. I'd never seen her lose her cool before, but she was definitely miffed at having ruined her outfit.

At the closet she took what seemed like an hour and a half choosing something else to wear. Then she picked up the blouse she'd thrown on the floor and stormed into the bathroom. I was praying she'd shut the door so I could make an escape, but she left it wide open, and I could see her working at the sink while I lay trapped beneath the bed. I had no choice but to stay where I was.

With every ounce of psychic power I could muster, I willed her to leave, but either I was a lousy sender or Holly was a crummy receiver. She came over and plunked herself down on the bed.

Don't look for the journal, I thought. *Do anything but look for the damned journal.* To my utter dismay, I felt her lean forward, turn around and reach under her pillow. I held my breath.

Suddenly she was on her feet, yanking back the covers, frantically searching for the book. She pulled open the drawer next to the bed and searched through the contents. When she got down on her hands and knees, I knew my time was up.

Just then, there was an urgent knock on the door, and Holly stood up. I'd been about to say something, and I had to force my mouth to close. My heart was beating so loudly I wouldn't have been surprised if the people in nearby cabins could hear it.

"Billie, what's up?" I was amazed at how quickly Holly was able to compose herself. Seconds earlier, she'd been ready to explode.

"Can I talk with you for a minute? It's kind of important."

"Sure, come on in."

"Uh, maybe it'd be better if you came over to my cabin. It won't take long."

I could tell Holly was thinking this over. Finally, she said, "Let me just grab my jacket."

When I heard the door close and their footsteps recede, I exhaled loudly. I'd been holding my breath for so long, my lungs ached.

I quickly placed the journal behind the bed so Holly would think it had inadvertently fallen down, then hurried to the door. Outside, the grounds were teeming with women! But there was nothing I could do about it. I slipped out, trying to blend in, my skin still clammy with fear.

An hour later I tracked down Billie and Allison. They were standing at the edge of the lake, deep in conversation.

"That was close," I said, squeezing Billie's shoulder.

"When Sabrina spilled her coffee all over Holly's silk blouse, I knew you'd be in trouble," she said. "Sure enough, she headed straight for her cabin. I had to think quick." Billie was wearing a pink and red cotton shirt over red bicycle shorts that would have looked silly on most people but looked somehow natural against her ebony skin.

"Two seconds later, I'd have been dead meat," I said. "She was getting down on her knees to look under the bed."

"Why?" Allison asked. The sun had caught the reddish gold highlights in her hair and reflected in her clear blue-green eyes. The slightly sunburned nose did nothing to dispel her beauty. I looked away and told them about the journal.

"God, don't you feel creepy going through other people's stuff? I'm glad I don't keep a diary."

"Thanks, Billie. It's not like I do it for cheap thrills." I paused. "You know, I've been driving myself crazy over these football notes. I mean, the obvious link is Reeva, right? Which could easily mean that someone's deliberately been trying to throw suspicion her way. You can't believe the number of disparaging remarks in Holly's journal regarding Reeva's obsession with football."

"Karen's almost as caught up in football as Reeva is," Billie said.

"Maybe so. My point is, if you were leaving notes to someone you were trying to kill, and everyone knew your favorite hobby was surfing, would you make constant references to waves?"

"So someone's framing Reeva?" Allison asked.

"I think someone might be making a feeble attempt to deflect suspicion from themselves by pointing in another direction. They might not have anything personal against Reeva. Maybe she's just an easy mark. Besides, Holly seems to be an equal-opportunity snob. She has bad things to say about everyone." The two of them looked pensive, obviously wondering what had been said about them.

"You really think it could be Holly?" Billy looked doubtful.

I sighed. "I don't know. But I do think it's time to take a more direct approach."

"What do you mean?" Allison asked.

"I think we should have Billie plant a story. It's time everyone knew the real reason I'm here." Billie looked at me, her eyes round. "I want you to tell each one, like they're the only one you're telling, that I've been investigating some attacks against Allison, and that I've figured out who the would-be killer is. I'm just waiting for the police to come so I can tell them who it is. Tell them I refused to tell either you or Allison the name. Can you do that?"

Billie's dark eyes narrowed and she glanced at Allison.

"That will make them come after you!" Allison exclaimed.

"You'll be the target," Billie said.

"That's the point. There're too many of them for me to chase. I need the killer to help me out a little."

"I wish you'd quit referring to her as a killer. So far, I'm still alive." Allison hugged herself as if sud-

143

denly chilled. She was wearing a satiny green blouse tucked into white knickers that stopped just above her lightly freckled knees. I couldn't help notice that the top three buttons of her blouse had been left open, revealing the pale swell of her breasts. It didn't help that the blouse was also nearly translucent. From where I was standing, the sun beat directly onto her cleavage. I made a point of studying a tree limb over her shoulder.

"Can you do it?" I asked Billie. She was still frowning.

"I can," she said. "I just don't know if I should."

"It's the only way," I said. "Besides, I'd much rather have them come after me when I'm expecting them, than to come after Allison when we're not."

Grudgingly, the two of them agreed that the plan was at least worth a shot.

The clouds had finally been chased off, and the day was turning into another beauty. The resort staff was setting up a barbecue down by the lake and women were already engaged in the various games set up along the shore. There were nets for volleyball and badminton, and courses laid on a grassy stretch for croquet and lawn bowling. Reeva was organizing another football game, and I was glad she had a whole bevy of new recruits. I'd had enough football to last me.

More than a dozen sailboats glided across the water, and brightly colored plastic paddleboats hugged the shore. Beds had been stripped of their blankets, and everywhere I looked, topless women were sprawled on the ground, tanning themselves. Off toward the pier, in a small cove, a number of women were swimming or floating on rafts. Steam rose off the water in vaporous puffs, and Allison explained that the cove's water was as warm as a heated pool.

"The cold water mixes with the natural hot springs running underneath the ground there, making the water temperature about eighty degrees. If you float out beyond those markers, though, you'll freeze your buns off. The rest of the lake is downright frigid."

"Who do you want me to talk to first?" Billie asked.

"Your choice," I said. "Just make sure they all get the same message. In fact, the sooner you tell them, the better."

"When I'm done, I'll come find you," she said. "Assuming one of them hasn't offed you both." She grinned, but Allison shivered, and folded her arms across her chest.

"You okay?" I asked, watching Billie march off in Karen's direction.

"Yeah, fine." She paused, then sighed. "Well, that's not entirely true. Actually, I'm pretty scared. About what you said earlier, well, I've been thinking."

"Allie, I had no right to pry into your life like that, and I have no business offering you advice. Hell, I can barely run my own life."

"Oh, you seem to be doing okay," she said, smiling. She started walking down toward the pier and I followed along.

"I know what you said was right, Cass. I need to get past what happened and get on with my life. Sometimes I think I've been using what happened as an excuse. But I'm nearly forty years old and it's time to be honest with myself. I don't want to spend the rest of my life having meaningless flings. If I even have a rest-of-my-life. I'm starting to feel as if whoever's trying to kill me is going to succeed."

"Is that supposed to be a vote of no confidence?" I was trying to lighten things up. She put her arm around my waist and squeezed my hip. When she felt the gun in my waistband, she pulled back. She stopped and looked at me.

"It's just a precaution, Allison. I'm sure I won't need it."

"I shouldn't be surprised. I mean, I did hire you to protect me. It's just that, I know it sounds stupid, but I don't want anyone to get hurt."

"Allie, someone's trying to hurt you. And as soon as Billie tells your stalker that I know who she is, she's probably going to want to hurt me. It's generally a good idea to be prepared in these situations. Okay?" I smiled, but her eyes still looked troubled.

"Maybe I should've taken your advice in the first place and not come up here."

Strong and sensible one second, frightened and vulnerable the next, Allison continued to amaze me with her mood swings. I put my arm around her shoulder and steered her toward the pier.

"We're going to find out who's doing this, and then you're going to get on with your life, okay?"

She nodded, leaning her head against my shoulder, letting her hand slip around my waist again, avoiding the thirty-eight nestled beneath my jacket. To anyone watching, we were just another loving couple strolling arm-and-arm along the lakeshore. Of course, as soon as Billie spread the word, there'd no longer be a need to pretend we were lovers. Still, I didn't move away, and neither did Allison. I had the feeling that all too soon this brief sense of calm was going to be shattered, and I wasn't all that anxious to let it go.

Chapter Sixteen

By three o'clock, Billie had told every last one of them, and already I was being treated differently. We were down by the barbecue grills eating hotdogs when Reeva pulled me aside. Her muscled arms glistened with sweat and her yellow flattop was plastered against her head. The football game had gone well, according to all reports. She was in a jubilant mood.

"Don't ask me how I know, okay? I just wanted you to know, if you need help, I'm here. And about last night, well, I'm sorry if me and Karen came on a little strong. I'd just gotten into an argument and had been hittin' the beer pretty good. I was in a bad mood, that's all." Reeva's gray eyes were looking everywhere but at me. She was clearly nervous about having this conversation. I got the feeling she wasn't used to apologizing.

"Well, I guess I wasn't in a very good mood either. Let's forget it, okay?"

"Your lip looks better," she said, her gaze shifting toward me, then darting away.

"It is." I couldn't figure out if Reeva was turning out to be a decent person, or if she was just trying to throw me off her trail.

"Well, anyway, if you need help or anything, just yell."

"I will, Reeva. Thanks."

No sooner had Reeva left me than Lacy Watkins came bouncing over. She had two beers in her hands and offered one to me. She'd even opened it, I noticed, smiling. I was getting the royal treatment.

"How are you, today, Cassidy?" she said, rocking forward on her toes.

"I'm just fine, Lacy. You?"

"Oh, I'm great. I just want you to know I think the world of Allison." She looked right at me, her buck-toothed grin making dimples in her cheeks.

"So do I, Lacy."

"I think you two make the cutest couple, too. Of course, I know someone who's not too happy about it, but . . ." She clearly wanted me to ask.

"Who's that?"

"I don't like to gossip," she said.

Sure you do, I thought. I waited.

"I think Sabrina's a little jealous, that's all. She's

kinda stuck on Allison. You probably haven't noticed."
You'd have had to be dead not to notice, I thought.

"I'm curious, Lacy. Can I ask you something personal?"

"Oh, sure." I walked down toward the water and she came bouncing along with me.

"Allison seems to have had quite an active love-life. Have the two of you ever dated? I hope this isn't too personal."

Lacy blushed and giggled. "I wish," she said. Realizing this might not be taken the right way, she quickly amended the statement. "I mean, now that you're together, it's out of the question, but, I mean, well, I think the world of Allison."

Clearly, Lacy wanted me to know she thought Allison was topnotch. Meaning she was trying very hard to convince me that she'd never lay a hand on Allison.

"I understand you're from a religious background, Lacy. Your dad was a preacher, right?"

Lacy stopped and whirled around, her eyes huge. "Who told you that?"

"Oh, *you* know. Word gets around. You still close with your family?"

Her face had taken on a pinkish hue and her eyes could have driven nails right through me. "My family and I are estranged," she said, her mouth tight.

"I'm sorry. I shouldn't have asked." This seemed to appease her somewhat. I really did feel bad. It was obvious I'd upset her.

"I shouldn't get so emotional about it." She took a sip of her beer. "It wasn't a pleasant situation. I just try not to think about it much, that's all. It happened a long time ago." She had begun bouncing on the balls of her feet again, her head bobbing nervously in rhythm with her body. If there'd been music, she could have been dancing.

"It must be difficult for you. Growing up with such strong beliefs, and then finding out you're gay. I'll bet that didn't go over very well with your father." I was sorry I had to push her so hard, but there was no other way I could think of to find out what I needed to know. Her left eye had begun to twitch. The vehemence in her voice surprised me.

"He hated it! Said I would burn in hell! Said the devil had entered my soul and I was rotting from the inside out! He tried to hospitalize me! Said it was God's will." Lacy began to cry, big, gulping sobs that racked her body.

I put my hand on her shoulder. "I'm sorry," I said.

"I believed in him!" Her words were muffled by sobs.

"God?" I asked.

She shook her head. "My father." Her eyes searched mine, begging me to understand. "Growing up, I thought he *was* God. Or at least God's direct messenger. All those people looking up to him each Sunday. He was always so sure about everything. I never doubted for a minute that he was right about things. I didn't realize that all that preaching about the wrath of God was really his own bigotry and hatred. Until it was directed at me." Her crying had become more subdued, her pain turning to anger.

"But you haven't lost your faith?" I asked.

She studied me behind reddened eyes. "I'm only now beginning to find it," she said. "It wasn't faith I had before. I was brainwashed. I did terrible things. My father's church did terrible things. I was part of that. Now I'm just trying to get clean."

I nodded, and noticed that for the first time since I'd met her, Lacy was standing still. She was watching me expectantly. "I'm glad you told me, Lacy. I needed to know."

"You thought I had something to do with what's happening to Allison?" She wiped her face on her shirttail.

"I knew you'd been arrested for what happened at the abortion clinic. That didn't seem to fit very well with your role in Women On Top."

"How do you know all this? I've never told anyone!"

"I'm a private investigator, Lacy. It's what I do."

She nodded, suddenly looking around us, her eyes narrowed. "Billie says someone's trying to kill Allison and you know who it is. Is it true?"

"I've got a pretty good idea," I said. This wasn't a total lie. I knew it wasn't Billie, and I thought Lacy's explanation of her past made sense. Besides, I didn't think she could fake all that hurt and anger. I felt almost sure I could cross Lacy off my list. Almost.

"Can you tell me?" she asked.

"Not yet," I said. "But keep your eyes and ears open. If you see or hear anything suspicious, let me know, okay?"

Her eyes brightened considerably and she rose up on the balls of her feet again, starting to bounce. "You can count on me, Cassidy," she said, grinning. And for some reason, I thought, heading back toward the others, I felt I really could.

Halfway back, we ran into the whole group walking toward us.

"Come on, we're going swimming!" Allison said, linking her arm through mine.

"I'm not wearing my suit," I protested.

"Who is?"

"Oh my. Our little Miss Chastity is shy!" Karen said. She wasn't calling me Cowgirl or John Girl today. But I wasn't sure "our little Miss Chastity" was an improvement. Allison led the way down to the water and people began disrobing.

"You can just wear your underthings," Sabrina said. "That's what I do."

"And most of us wish you wouldn't," Reeva said. Everyone laughed, including Fay who had stripped to a full-piece black swimsuit. To my surprise, without the bulky sweatshirt she usually hid beneath, Fay's body was voluptuous. She seemed to sense people staring at her and quickly dove into the water.

"What about you, Holly?" I asked.

She looked at me, a sly smile on her lips. Then, without warning, she lifted her shirt above her head and flashed her breasts at me. She was wearing an orange bikini under her clothes. Which figured, I thought. Holly wasn't the type to expose anything she didn't want to.

The cove was protected from the breeze by a rocky outcropping along its east bank that rose up in jagged black formations and stretched several hundred feet into the lake. The afternoon sun was still strong and warmed the sand along the shore. The scent of sulphur wafted from the water, but not nearly as noticeably as from the hot tubs behind the cabins. A dozen or so women lazed on floating rafts, while others swam and played in the water. I was pretty sure that one couple, way off by the rocks, was making love. They were trying to be discreet about it, but I recognized something about the way they moved, and suddenly missed Maggie more than I could bear.

"Penny for your thoughts," Allison whispered. She had pulled off her shirt and was stepping out of her knickers.

I shrugged, looking away, but no matter where I turned, I saw half-naked women. As promised, Sabrina had stripped to her silken panties and bra. They were pink and transparent, somehow sexier than if she had been totally naked. When she dipped into the water and stood back up, the wet silk clung to her body, and there wasn't a woman there who didn't take notice. Somehow I didn't think my cotton briefs would have the same effect.

I pulled off my clothes, carefully concealing my gun in my shirt, which wasn't easy to do. Holly was watching me, a thin smile crossing her lips. I think she thought I was overly shy about disrobing in front of them. I lay my bundle on a flat rock and dove into the water. It wasn't that I didn't like skinny-dipping, I thought. I just didn't usually do it with strangers.

Despite my misgivings, the water felt wonderful. Allison had said the water was about eighty degrees, and maybe it was. Every now and then I crossed a spot that felt closer to ninety, only to cross one that couldn't have been warmer than sixty. It resulted in a pleasant succession of goosebumps followed by marvelous warmth.

"Here. You can share my raft," Allison said. Her

head and elbows rested on the lime-green raft, while her legs bicycled beneath. I took the side of the raft opposite her and we bicycled together.

"I think Lacy's safe," I murmured, knowing that voices carry over water.

She sighed. "Well, that's two down, five to go."

Reeva, Karen, Sabrina, Fay and Holly. I let their images swirl in my head, hoping one of them would suddenly become illuminated, little arrows pointing at her, saying, "This is the one!" Unfortunately, nothing happened. Allison touched my foot with her toe, but I was too deep in thought to look up. She let her foot slide up my calf, trying to get my attention. I knew she was doing it, but I needed to concentrate. There was something about one of the women I wasn't remembering. When I felt her toes brush against my thigh, I jerked. She was grinning wickedly, and I realized my face had gone crimson.

"Jeez, I thought I lost you there."

"I was trying to think," I said, humiliated at the fluttering in my stomach.

"You've got great powers of concentration, I see." She had obviously noticed my blushing and wasn't going to let it slide.

"I'm going for a swim," I said. I pushed myself off the raft and dove under the water, heading for the rocky edge of the cove. I pumped hard, pushing myself, slicing through the water, letting the tension out with each stroke. I kept my eyes open to avoid the many women I passed. What was it that had slipped my mind? Something significant, I was almost sure. But the thought of Allison's foot against my calf erased any chance I had of regaining my focus. When I reached the rocky cliff, I turned toward the buoys that ringed the outer edge of the cove and pushed myself harder.

I was almost to the outer edges, breathing hard, when something bumped against my leg. I felt a sharp sting but didn't stop. I'd probably nicked myself on one of the protruding rocks. Angry at myself for the way my body kept responding to Allison's advances, I welcomed the pain. In fact, it was the thought of Allison's advances that kept me from worrying about the pain.

I was panting by the time I reached the white buoys bobbing on the surface near the demarcation of the cove. The water along the cliff face was dark and cloudy with mud. I grabbed onto the rope and rested against the rocky edge, catching my breath.

Suddenly, the stinging sensation in my leg spread upward. My whole left side started to tingle and my left foot became completely numb. I looked around but no one in the water seemed to be looking in my direction. I started to call out, but my mouth had somehow lost its ability to form sounds. Panicking, I managed a pathetic moan.

I'm in trouble, here, I thought, as I grappled for some explanation. *Think!* I berated myself. *You have to get out of the water!* I tried to scream, but the sounds came out as unrecognizable grunts. Slowly, I dragged myself up onto the rocky outcropping.

The black rock was both slippery and jagged as I struggled to pull myself up onto the ledge. I felt skin tearing but didn't care. As long as I could rest with my head out of the water, I'd be okay. I hoped. I wasn't really sure. I just knew I needed to get out of the lake.

When I found a crack in the rock and dug my

fingers into it, I used every ounce of strength I had to position myself. With a great heaving sob, I draped myself across the uneven slab, my feet still dangling in the water. I lay there listening to my heart pound in my head. My mouth was dry, my tongue thick. I tried to look at my leg to see the wound, but my vision blurred as quickly as my ability to speak. Had I been stung by something poisonous? A fresh-water jellyfish? Was there such a thing? I couldn't make my mind work clearly.

Suddenly, something pierced through the numbness in my ankle. It felt like someone tickling me with barbed wire. I wanted to turn my head to see what was causing this new sensation, but my neck wouldn't budge. My eyes were open, but I could only see what was right in front of me, and even that was fuzzy. My fingers dug into the rock, frantically clinging for safety, but with a terror I hadn't felt before, I realized I was being pulled back down into the water.

My eyes were open, seeing the safety of dry land slip away. I wanted to reach out, to save myself, but my grip was useless; my voice box emitted weak mewling sounds instead of the screams I intended. I felt the rock cut into my cheek, gouging the side of my head as I was dragged across the jagged rock. I smelled blood even as my ears filled with water and I sank below the murky surface. My arms and legs were dead weight, dormant limbs weighing me down. As foggy as my mind was, I knew with utter despair that it was the only part of me still functional.

So this was it. The thing had finally come to get me. I struggled to see through the muddy water but couldn't. I opened my mouth to scream as it dragged me under but something stopped me from letting the water in. Even so, the thing was sucking the air right out of my lungs. It was just like the dream — dark and sinister. It needed to be stopped. But with my arms and legs practically paralyzed, how was I supposed to defeat this thing? When I tried to lash out, it was as if the thing were laughing. My head pounded, my ears buzzed and a sob built up in my chest. My arms and legs belonged to someone else.

I tried to clear my head. This was not a dream, I told myself. Was it? I hoped it was. No, it wasn't. I strained to see the thing pulling me downward. It was too murky. I realized that it wasn't just the water that was clouded, it was my vision. And then I started not to care.

This is how it's supposed to happen, I thought. Why else the dream, over and over? This thing was my destiny. And then I thought of Maggie. She would care. She would not want me to give into this thing.

Something inside me, deep down, further down than I'd ever gone, snapped. It was angry. Livid. It lifted my right arm, made me reach out through the water and grab onto the only thing I could. My fingers became claws, and the claws connected. As I was drowning, I had the absurd satisfaction of knowing that at least my killer would be badly marked, branded for what she was.

Suddenly, inexplicably, the thing let go. Almost unconscious, I floated upward, some other force propelling me to the surface. My mouth opened, gulping air. The light was blinding, the pain in my head unbearable. And then darkness, sweet, peaceful darkness, engulfed me.

I didn't know how much time had passed. It could have been seconds or days. Or a lifetime. All I know is that, when I heard the words, "She's come to!" I knew I was still alive.

"Help me roll her over. One, two, three. Easy now. There you go. Good girl." Allison's voice was calm, soothing, but a million miles away. One of us was in a tunnel.

"Doesn't anyone have something we can stop this blood with?"

"Sabrina's underwear," the person holding me said. It sounded like they were speaking from outer space. There was more dialogue, but I drifted back down, thinking that if I kept my eyes open underwater I might be able to see the thing's face. I tried to tell myself I was no longer underwater, but I wasn't sure.

Allison's voice interrupted the dream. "Can you hear me, Cass?" She held something soft against my cheek. As disoriented as I was, some cognizant part of me understood that she was dabbing blood off of my face with Sabrina's underwear. I managed a weak smile.

"I know this hurts, honey. I'm sorry." Apparently my smile had come off more like a grimace.

"Wha' hap—" I tried. My tongue was as thick as cotton batting. I was vaguely aware of bare breasts against my back. Whoever held me in her arms was naked. It was nice, and I started to drift back down.

"Did you see who it was?" Allison whispered into my ear. I tried to shake my head. Big mistake. I was treated to a dazzling light display. Suddenly, I felt nauseous.

"Don't move around so much," Allison said.

"Gon' be sick," I managed. She understood. Cradling my head with her hands, she helped me roll over so that I didn't vomit on myself. I sensed the others watching, but I was too sick to care. After what seemed an eternity, Allison helped me sit up. The person who'd been holding me finally moved away. I looked up and nearly choked. Reeva smiled shyly.

"Better?" Allison asked. Carefully, I nodded. In truth, I felt quite a bit better. My vision was starting to clear, and the ringing in my ears was down to a mild roar. The numbness on the left side of my body had retreated, leaving a pin-prickling sensation behind. I could feel my foot again. Things were definitely looking up.

"We've got to get you out of this cold air," Allison said. For the first time, I realized that I was stark naked, and that more than half a dozen women, some of whom I didn't recognize, had been standing over me for who knew how long. I had a sudden and intense desire to cover myself, but looking around, I realized that almost everyone else was nearly as naked as I was. Except, of course, Holly. Where had she been when they needed something to soak up the blood with, I wondered. Not that her bikini would have done much more good than Sabrina's underpants. Still . . .

"Do you know what happened?" Reeva asked.

"Got stung with something," I said. My mouth was starting to work again. "Right here." I indicated my leg. "I lost consciousness. I think someone pulled me into the water."

"Someone tried to drown you, is more like it," Reeva said. "Did a pretty good job of it too. I heard a scream, and when I looked up, you were being dragged under. I wasn't that far away, but by the time I got there, you were damn near drowned. I only wish I could've seen who it was, but the water was just too muddy. By the time I reached you, they were already gone. As it is, you're lucky to be alive with all that bleeding."

It was true. The side of my head was slick with my own blood, and it had pooled in my ear. Sabrina's panties were already soaked through.

"Will she need stitches?" Billie asked.

"Just a few," Allison said. "Head wounds bleed a lot. It looks worse than it is."

"I'll be fine," I said. Since I'd thrown up, I was feeling amazingly well. The cut on my head wasn't nearly as bad as my reaction to whatever had stung me. I told Allison this and she examined my leg.

"It doesn't look like a bite mark. More like you got stuck with something, although there is a second mark. Like whatever got you here, went out right here." When she touched the spot, my leg involuntarily jerked. "You say you lost consciousness before you were dragged under?"

I nodded. I was pretty sure that was the sequence of events, but my mind was still foggy. I was having trouble separating what had happened from the dream. Then for the first time, I noticed four jagged welts running down Reeva's cheek, still oozing blood. I stared at them, clenching my right fist against my stomach, wondering. It was so hard to separate the dream from reality. The thing had been there, and

I'd reached out and clawed something. There must be skin under my nails to prove it. And later, Reeva had cradled me in her arms. Had she been my protector? Or had she been the one to drag me under? No doubt if I asked, she'd say I scratched her as she pulled me to safety.

"You ready to travel?" Allison asked. I nodded and let them help me to my feet. Standing up brought on a whole new wave of nausea, but it passed relatively quickly. They eased me into the water and guided me across the cove. By the time my feet hit dry sand, I was shivering.

"Here are your clothes, Cassidy," Lacy said, running down to meet us. When she handed me the bundle, my thirty-eight dropped to the ground. Everyone stopped dead and looked from the gun to me.

"Thanks, Lacy." It took me forever, but I was never more glad to get dressed. I slipped the gun into my waistband and pulled my shirt over it, trying to appear nonchalant, but my body still trembled and my coordination was off. The other women were throwing on their clothes as well and no one was talking.

It was Reeva who finally broke the awkward silence. "I think we need to talk," she said, staring intently at Allison. "Obviously, there's something going on and I think everyone has a right to know what's happening."

"I agree," Allison said. "It's time to bring things out in the open. But right now, I need to get Cassidy over to the first-aid station where I can stitch her up. We'll set up a time to talk, I promise."

On wobbly legs, still holding Sabrina's panties to my head, I walked between Allison and Billie all the way to the lodge. I let them support me when I stumbled, thinking it was nice, in a strange way, to be cared for. Sometimes you have to come close to death, I thought, to really appreciate the simple pleasure of being alive.

Chapter Seventeen

Seeing Allison in her role as a doctor gave me new insight into her. She was decisive and focused, without ever losing her patience. Her touch was gentle, yet deft. She used soothing tones but there was no doubt about who was in charge. Most impressive were her eyes. I'd seen them as sexy and kind. I'd seen them filled with humor and with fear. But I'd never once seen the intensity they held while she was stitching my head. Over the years I'd heard about athletes entering what they called the "zone," a certain level of intensity in which, no matter what they did, they couldn't miss. Pitchers in the midst of throwing a no-hitter sometimes had that look. Allison had it now. It reminded me of what Billie said about Allison making love.

"I don't think you got stung," she said when she'd finished cleaning me up.

"Me neither," I said. "What *do* you think?"

"The second mark on your leg looks like an exit wound. The size of both is consistent with that of a hypodermic needle. My guess is that someone tried to jab your leg, but because of your movement they weren't able to get a clean shot. The needle entered here, then exited right here. Whatever they were shooting you with was potent enough to knock you nearly unconscious, despite the fact that most of it never got into your system. Had they managed to hit a vein, I imagine the dosage would've been enough to kill you."

"That's a cheery thought," I said.

Allison shuddered. "It's not a joking matter, Cassidy. You're as much a target now as I am."

"What do you think it could be? I mean, what causes these symptoms?" I described them for her as best I could.

She shook her head smiling. "The possibilities are endless. There are drugs, including over-the-counter, prescription and illegal, that could bring on these symptoms. There are plenty of poisons, including industrial, household and natural materials that could have similar effects. The venom from certain spiders and snakes is also a possibility. Not to mention deadly plants like foxglove and certain mushrooms. If you know what you're doing, it wouldn't be hard to concoct a lethal solution."

I thought of Holly's book on mushrooms and wondered. But she wasn't the only one who knew about poisonous mushrooms. After I'd told Reeva's friend, Harriet, the truth about what she'd thought were morels, a lot of people knew, including Reeva. And something that had been bothering me about Karen for a long time came to me so suddenly I blinked.

The day before, when I'd searched Karen's wallet, I'd been so focused on the fact that Allison had been cut out of the picture that I hadn't given the other pictures their due. One of them had been of Karen in the classroom with two students standing in front of a chalkboard. On the board had been a chart of the periodic tables, indicating that she was standing in a science lab. Karen said she was a P.E. teacher, but that didn't mean it was the only subject she taught. Suddenly I was curious about the range of Karen's areas of expertise. Science teachers tend to know quite a bit about mixing chemical substances and about how they might affect the human system.

I tried to picture Karen dropping a bee box through Allison's window, and the image fit. I could see her lacing Allison's milk and doctoring her pâte. She was friends with Reeva, so maybe she knew enough about cars to cut the brake lines too. She probably wouldn't have too much trouble filling a hypodermic needle and jabbing it into my leg. But why hadn't I found the needle when I searched the room? And why would she have one in the first place? I ran these thoughts by Allison and she listened patiently.

"I have needles in my bag," she said. "In fact, even among the meager supplies I brought along, there are no doubt a few things that, used the right way, could kill someone. I suppose someone could've broken in and helped herself." She started searching through her bag, her brows furrowed. "I can't be sure, but it's possible I'm missing a needle. I don't see anything else that jumps out at me. I guess I should've left the bag in my room instead of here, but I wanted to be able to get to it quickly in case of an emergency. How's that feel?"

She held up a small rectangular mirror for me to examine the stitches on the side of my head. She'd shaved a tiny patch of hair, which didn't do much for my looks, but other than that I felt pretty good. The cut along my cheek was superficial, and after cleaning it thoroughly, she'd covered it with a small bandage. I looked worse than I felt. The effects from whatever I'd been stuck with seemed to have worn off almost completely.

"I guess I'm going to have to talk to your whole staff," I said. "We certainly succeeded in flushing out the stalker by making everyone think I knew who she was, but by now they all have to know that I don't have a clue."

"Can't we set a trap or something?" She was still standing above me, her reddish gold hair catching the light through the window. It was nearly dusk, and the setting sun threw an orangeish glow across her features. She was lovely, I thought. I was in no hurry to leave.

Suddenly, I had an idea. "Let's do this," I said. "You go with Billie to dinner tonight. Tell the whole group that I've taken a turn for the worse, that I'm very disoriented and confused and that as my doctor, you've ordered complete bed rest until morning. Tell them we'll plan to hold a meeting with everyone tomorrow morning at breakfast, when I'm feeling better. Tell them I haven't told you what I know, but that you think I've identified the killer. Whatever you do, don't leave Billie's side. In fact, maybe you should plan to spend the night in her cabin. Just to be safe."

"You think they'll come after you?"

"It's worth a shot. God knows they did it once. If they think I'm planning to expose them in the morning, it's a good bet they'll try again, especially if they think I'm incapacitated."

"It just might work," she said. "But I don't want to leave you alone. After dinner, I'm coming back. But I'll make sure everyone thinks I'm going to Billie's. We'll make a show of wanting to be alone. Now that everyone understands that the thing between you and me was for show, they won't think twice about Billie and me spending time together. As far as anyone's concerned, they'll think you're all alone and an easy target."

"You sure you want to come back?" I asked.

"Yeah, why?"

"Well as long as you're coming, you think you could sneak me some food? I'm starving."

"Has anyone ever checked you for tapeworms?" she asked, laughing. "I could do it now. I think I've got an endoscope somewhere in my bag. It only hurts for a while."

I punched her on the arm and followed her to the door where Billie was still standing guard outside.

"You better let us help you, in case anyone's watching. Try to look dazed and confused," Allison said.

"That should be easy. I'll just pretend I'm you." I smiled sweetly, and Allison took my arm, pinching my biceps in the process. Billie took my other arm and the three of us made our way back to the cabin slowly. We hardly saw a soul, though. Apparently everyone was already in the lodge for dinner.

While Allison and Billie were at dinner, I spent more time working on my notes, updating motives and opportunities for the five women I still suspected. The scratches on Reeva's face concerned me. She said she'd seen me slipping into the water and rescued me. Apparently I gouged her in the process. But wasn't that a convenient story? Why hadn't she been able to see who was pulling me down? The water had been muddy, but how long could a person stay under? She would've seen my attacker when she surfaced, unless she merely joined the rest of the women swimming over to help. Maybe when the others saw what was happening and came to investigate, Reeva had been forced to quit what she was really doing and pretend to pull me to safety. The situation was mind-boggling, and my head was hurting again.

I was still at work when Allison returned bearing a tray laden with food. Billie was with her, grinning with mischief.

"Sustenance," Billie said, pulling a bottle of Cabernet Sauvignon from under her bright red jacket. "I lifted it when no one was looking."

"I thought you two were going to make people think you were going to Billie's place," I said, eyeing the food. The plate was piled high with meat loaf, steamed broccoli and mashed potatoes covered with gravy. There were three pieces of chocolate cream pie on the tray as well. Comfort food, I thought, digging in. A perfect choice. Billie poured the wine and came to sit at the little table across from me, helping herself to a piece of pie.

"We told them we were bringing you a sick tray, but that you probably wouldn't be awake enough to eat," Billie said. "Then, when I was pretty sure everyone could hear me, I asked Allison if she wanted to come hot-tubbing tonight at my place. We gave each other a few long, meaningful glances that I'm sure no one could miss, and Allison nibbled my neck in the dessert line. Tonight was one of those buffet thingies."

"You sure no one poisoned this?" I asked, holding my fork an inch from my mouth. It was too late anyway. I'd already eaten half the mashed potatoes.

"If they did, there's gonna be a lot of sick people. We took it from the same dish as everyone else."

"What did you tell them?" I asked Allison. She was nibbling at her pie, sipping the red wine thoughtfully.

"Pretty much what you said. Lacy's very concerned about you and offered to come sit with you tonight. So did Fay. Believe it or not, Reeva seemed concerned too. Sabrina's ticked off about her underpants, I think. Which naturally Holly found hilarious. Karen was pretty quiet. When we left, she and Sabrina were dancing. All anyone can talk about is the football notes and what they mean."

"You think they bought the setup?" I asked.

"Hard to tell. I guess the only way we'll know for sure is if someone comes after you."

"I think we should all just go to my cabin," Billie said. "It's stupid to lie around waiting for someone to come kill you. They can't keep missing forever."

"This may be their last chance," I said. "At any rate, they may think it is. Besides, I've got my gun."

"A lot of good it did you today," Billie pointed out.

I reached over and poured myself more wine. "It'll be right beside me tonight."

"And I'll be right next door. In fact, I think we should change the camera so that it shoots into your room," Allison said.

"Camera?" Billie asked. Allison explained about my video cam.

"Let's just keep it how it is," I said. "Don't forget, Allie, they may be coming after me now, but you're still the primary target. My guess is, if they do try something tonight, it may involve both of us."

"God, this is so stupid!" Billie exploded. "You two are sitting around here talking as if you're discussing a tea party while some sicko is plotting your death. Can't we at least stand guard outside?"

"If they see someone outside, they won't come. The whole point is to set a trap. If we don't find out who it is now, we may never know. Which means they'll be free to try again and again. This is our best chance right now."

Billie heaved a huge sigh and helped herself to the rest of Allison's pie. Allison poured them both more wine.

"So I'm supposed to do what? Lie awake and worry? I hate this!"

Allison put her arm around Billie's shoulder and drew her toward her. She kissed her on the forehead. "Cass knows what she's doing, Billie. If everything goes right, this whole damn mess will be over."

I only hoped she was right. If not, I was afraid I

171

was running out of trump cards. And I didn't have any aces up my sleeve. My only protection was the thirty-eight under my waistband, already witnessed by everyone involved. Not the way I would have planned it, but then, so far, nothing had really gone according to plan. I hadn't even gotten a chance to use my binocular-strength sunglasses, and with no phones, my portable recorder was useless. So much for high-tech surveillance, I thought. But who knew? Maybe things were about to change for the better.

Chapter Eighteen

It was dark. The clouds had slunk back over the mountain and lay like a blanket overhead, blocking out the moon and stars. My room was still. I'd been lying in wait, listening hard for hours. My muscles were rigid and tense. When the bathroom door creaked open, I grabbed for the gun beneath my pillow.

"It's just me, Cass. I couldn't sleep. Did I wake you?"

I fell back down, burying my head in the pillow.

My heart was pounding. Allison came and sat on the edge of the bed.

"I don't think they're coming," she said.

"What time is it?"

"About three. They'd have come by now, don't you think?"

"Probably. Why don't you get some sleep. I'm awake anyway," I said.

"I couldn't sleep if I wanted to. I heard you tossing around in here a while ago. Why don't you let *me* stay awake, and *you* try to get some sleep. Here, just try to relax." Her hands slid across my shoulders, her fingers probing gently into the muscles, finding the aches beneath the surface. "Does that hurt?" she asked, positioning herself above my back.

"A little," I admitted. I had exhausted every muscle in my body trying to pull her up the cliff the day before. She dug her fingers into the sore spots, manipulating them until I began to relax. I realized I'd been holding my breath and clenching my fists, and I forced myself to let go.

"That's better," she said, moving down to knead the tense back muscles. She slid her hands under my T-shirt. Her fingers deftly found the tender areas, and although she was gentle, there was a ruthlessness in her touch. When I gasped, she eased up and concentrated on another, equally tender area. I gave up resisting and let myself enjoy the exquisite pain. Until she'd started to work on me, I hadn't realized just how sore I'd been. For the first time in days, I felt my body start to relax.

As she moved to my hips. I wished I'd worn more

than just my underwear and T-shirt to bed. It was more than I usually wore, but I'd been expecting trouble. Still, with Allison's hands kneading my buttocks, I was suddenly self-conscious. Before I could resist, she moved downward and I let out an involuntary moan.

"Tender?" she asked, probing my thigh.

I nodded into my pillow, trying to ignore the pain, let alone the other sensations I'd begun to feel as she rhythmically pressed me against the bed, her fingers pushing into my flesh. Kneading my calf, she then began working her way up my other leg. I found myself holding my breath again as she crept closer to what had become an increasingly urgent throbbing.

"You're still tense," she said, cupping my thigh with both hands, using her thumbs to dig deeper. The back of her one hand brushed against the elastic of my underwear and she quickly moved away. I shuddered, my face burning. Again her fingers brushed against me, and this time I knew it hadn't been accidental.

"Allison," I croaked. My voice was embarrassingly husky.

"Shhh . . ." she murmured. Her own voice sounded as bad as mine. She had her hands on both thighs now, pushing, kneading, her thumbs just tracing the elastic of my underpants, back and forth, so softly while she pounded at my legs — well not my legs, really, and not just the elastic, but closer, her thumbs nearly touching each other and the damp heat beneath the thin cotton, until, heart pounding, every part of me throbbing, I cried out.

"Please!" It was all I could manage. My voice

175

shattered the quiet. Allison stopped moving. She pulled her hands away. Her breathing was as ragged as my own.

When at last she spoke, her voice was almost a whisper. "Please don't stop? Or please leave me alone?" she finally asked. She sounded as if, either way, she might cry.

"Please go back to your room, Allie. If you care about me at all, please do that right now."

I felt her body brush against mine as she slid off the bed. Every fiber of my being pulsated. I knew she was standing above me, but I couldn't bring myself to look at her.

"You must love her very much," she said at last. I nodded into my pillow. "I'm sorry," she said. "It won't happen again." At the door, she paused. "I hope she knows how lucky she is."

I didn't breathe until I heard both doors close behind her.

It was nearly light before I really let myself fall asleep, and when I did, the dreams haunted me. There was no evil thing dragging me underwater for once, but even so, my heart was pounding when I awoke. It had started with Maggie, her deep green eyes smiling down at me while she did things I can't describe. But the eyes turned turquoise and the black curls gave way to reddish gold waves. When I realized it was Allison I was making love with, my body jerked awake.

It was later than I thought. The sun was stuck somewhere behind an ominous gathering of thunderheads, and the sky was eerily dark. Trees rustled in the breeze, and I hugged my jacket around me as I stepped out onto the porch. I wasn't looking forward to seeing Allison and was relieved that she'd apparently already gone to breakfast. I peeked through her windows to verify her departure. Apparently, she hadn't been anxious to see me either.

I knew they were all expecting me to meet with them this morning, supposedly to identify the would-be killer. But since I couldn't exactly do that, I went back inside and rummaged around in the small refrigerator until I found something to eat. A lot of people would have turned their nose up at cheese and salami for breakfast, but it was my guess they probably hadn't tried it.

I sat down with my feast and a cup of coffee to try to hammer out a plan. My trap hadn't worked, and if I couldn't make my assailant come after me, I was going to have to go after her. Since I didn't know which one to go after, I'd have to go after them all. I wrote their names on a napkin and tore it into five squares. Holly, Fay, Karen, Reeva and Sabrina. I shuffled the squares, rearranging them in various orders, trying to decide.

Whoever had stuck me with the needle, must have carried it with her into the water. Reeva and Karen had both been naked. Could Holly or Fay have hidden the needle in their swimsuits? I doubted that Sabrina could have concealed it in her silky underwear. We wouldn't have missed it. On the other hand, almost everyone had taken one of the rafts to float around on. The needle could have easily been concealed inside one of the little grooves, and no one would have noticed. And there were other possibilities, I realized, letting my mind roam.

Karen had been wearing a pair of sunglasses. Maybe she'd hidden the needle inside her glasses case and carried it with her. I supposed, if someone had been really desperate, they could've encapsulated it and inserted it vaginally. God knows we'd all read enough prison stories to know that trick. Even so, I shuddered.

I realized, dejected, that any one of them could have carried the needle with them. I took out my notes, studying them for something I'd missed.

Holly, as Women On Top's financial advisor, had the best motive, I thought. She alone knew of Allison's fortune and, presumably, her will. The way she always seemed to be watching and waiting, reminded me of a cat toying with a mouse.

For that matter, Fay Daniels always seemed to be watching, too, but as the newest member of the group, and one who might be unsure of her sexual orientation, maybe this was to be expected, but for some reason it bothered me that she and Allison were born in the same town. I kept forgetting to ask Allison about it and made myself another note to do so.

Karen, I now realized, was smitten with Sabrina, who in turn fawned over Allison. From Karen's dark looks and remarks, I sensed real hostility toward Allison. In fact, from the moment she thought Allison and I were lovers, her demeanor toward me had changed from friendly to downright ugly. Was jealousy enough of a motive? I already knew she had the means and opportunity.

Reeva, the organization's vice president, had her own motive: she envied Allison's popularity and position of power. She was also the one most adamant about the officers being paid more. With Allison out of the picture, and with the money willed to WOT, there was a good chance Reeva could get everything she wanted. I kept flashing back to the moment when I realized it was Reeva cradling me in her arms. Was she my protector? Or a clever psychopath?

Finally, there was Sabrina, the group's grant writer who was obviously love-sick over Allison. Her mood swings, past history of arson, and use of meds all pointed to emotional instability, to say the least. She came off as timid, but watching the way she played football, I knew she could be a relentless adversary. Of all of them, Sabrina's personality fit best with the profile of a stalker.

I sighed. Anyone of them could be trying to kill Allison. Suddenly, my joke about them all being in on it together, didn't seem so funny. I was getting desperate. It was already Thursday and I wasn't that much closer to knowing the truth. And I had a nagging feeling that if I didn't find out soon, the would-be killer would eventually succeed.

I may have managed to kick Allison out of my room last night, but she had definitely wormed her way into my heart. She wasn't just a client anymore. It had gotten personal. Even if the attacker hadn't come after me, I knew I'd be going after her with more than a professional detachment. Which could be dangerous.

I tossed the little squares of paper in the air and snatched one before they could land. I smiled. Holly McIntyre's name lay crumpled in my palm.

Chapter Nineteen

"We missed you at breakfast," Holly said, blocking the doorway to her cabin. She was dressed in navy velour sweats and Reeboks, her blond hair tied back with a matching navy scarf. She looked ready for a jog along Hollywood Boulevard.

"May I come in?" I asked.

There was a brief hesitation, then she shrugged and stepped aside. "You seem to be feeling better. It's amazing what the powers of love can accomplish. Or is it true that you and Allison have just been play-acting at this little love-game?" She was leaning nonchalantly against her dresser, her legs crossed at the ankles. She stifled a yawn.

I ignored the question, went to her bed, reached behind her pillow and pulled out her journal.

"Hey!" she shouted, rushing to grab it. I held it out of her reach and pushed my other hand against her chest, keeping her at arm's length. She swatted angrily at my arm, and her face darkened.

"Sit down," I said calmly.

"You have no right!"

"I'll tell you what I've got," I said. "I've got a pretty good idea why you'd like to see Allison Crane dead. And I've got reason to believe you not only have the motive, but you've had the means and opportunity to kill her. And," I said, waving the book in the air, "I've got your journal. Now sit down."

She slumped onto the bed, her brown eyes fuming. "You were in my cabin," she accused. "You went through my things. I knew someone had moved my journal!"

I began thumbing through it. "Tell me something, Holly. Do you hate everyone, or just the people you know?"

"I don't hate." She paused, then met my eyes. "To hate, you need to feel. I don't allow myself to feel very often. Obviously you need to read a little more closely. I simply report what I see."

"Jeez. I'd hate to see what you'd write if you *did* hate. No feelings, huh? Must be a pretty grim life, Holly. How do you get your kicks? Besides nice clothes, I mean."

She rolled her eyes, reminding me of an adolescent. For someone who didn't feel, she was exhibiting all kinds of anger.

"Here's an interesting passage." I read aloud. " 'Allison Crane thinks she's some kind of fuck-goddess. Ms. Passion Unlimited. Why doesn't she just buy herself a vibrator and spare the rest of us her pathetic extremes?' " I looked up. "You ever find yourself the recipient of these extremes?"

"Have *you*?" she retorted.

Touche, I thought. One point for Holly.

"Seems to me, for someone who claims not to feel, you've got an awful lot of anger. Let's see. Oh, here's a delightful passage: 'I'd like to yank Fay by that ridiculous ponytail and swing her against the wall. The way she follows Allison around is enough to make me puke.' Oh and let's see. You call Reeva 'a bull dyke with bad hair,' Lacy 'the Bouncing-Wonder,' Karen 'a robotic reptile' and Sabrina, let me find this. Yes, here it is; 'a squirmy psychopath with excessive hormones.' Seems like you've got a thing against hormones, Holly. But then again, I suppose hormones might actually interfere with your quest for numbness. Tell me, what'd you do with the book on mushrooms? Hide it after you finished making your little Hollytov Cocktail?"

"Is that supposed to be funny? Forgive me for not laughing."

"Where is it?" I wasn't smiling.

"I lent it to someone. Anything else you want to know?"

"Who?"

"You're the detective. Find out."

"Tell me this, Holly. I'm just curious. Why do you stay with Women On Top? It's clear you like no one. And I don't see anyone falling over herself to get close to you. What's in it for you? Besides Allison's money."

"What's that supposed to mean?" She had folded her arms in front of her and was sitting cross-legged on the bed.

"I think you know what I'm talking about. Allison's inheritance."

Holly stared at me for a moment, then tilted her head back and laughed. "You think I know something about something that I don't," she said. "God, if you're the only hope Allison has, she may as well kiss it good-bye." Her laugh was genuine. Her eyes were even tearing.

"Cut the act, Holly. I've already talked to your ex," I lied. "Hard to believe you've ever been with someone, but she just happens to be the one who drew up Allison's will, as you and I both know. She talked to you about the money. You know how much, and you also know that once Women On Top gets it, you'll have control of it." I hoped my lying eyes weren't giving me away. All I had was Allison's earlier mention that her attorney, Kate Monroe, had been Holly's lover. The rest was pure conjecture.

"You're full of shit!" she spat. "God, I can't believe this. Kate Monroe never told me anything. And she wouldn't lie, either. I think you're the one who needs to cut the act, Cassidy. If that's even your name."

With a sinking feeling, I realized she might be telling the truth. "Who'd you lend the book to?" I asked.

"Reeva," she said. "Are you through?"

"For now, Holly." I tossed her the journal. "You're a good writer," I said. "And an intelligent, good-looking woman. If you ever get your shit together, you might be a decent person. Think about therapy, Holly. It's time to let some of that anger out." I hoped I sounded as patronizing as I felt.

I shut the door behind me just as the journal slammed into it, missing my head by a fraction of an inch. I smiled. It looked like the anger was starting to let itself out after all.

Outside, the clouds continued to crowd together, bulbous and purple. A distant rumble rolled through the gorge from the west, promising thunder and lightning. I pulled my jacket close and dug another square out of my pocket. I peeked at it, then headed for Karen's cabin.

I nearly collided with Lacy, who was jogging up the path.

"Cassidy! They said you were feeling better. Are you coming?"

"Coming where?" I asked.

"It's Thursday. The big race!"

"In this weather?" I looked skyward.

"They say it won't rain for another few hours. We should all be back by then. Come on!"

So that's what Holly had been dressed for, I thought. "What time does it start?"

"About fifteen minutes. Everyone's already over at the lodge. I just came to get Holly. She said she'd enter this year."

I looked down. I was wearing my gray sweats and tennies, and I'd strapped my shoulder holster over the sweatshirt where I could reach it easily under my windbreaker. I hadn't wanted to interview my suspects empty-handed. Now I was glad I'd brought it along.

"I'll be there," I said, wondering if she'd be able to talk Holly into racing. I was afraid I may have dampened her good spirits.

The idea of putting my body through a race was not appealing. My thighs still ached and my arms were weak with fatigue. I felt as if I'd had the flu and now that the scrape on my cheek was discoloring, I looked almost as bad as I felt. But if Allison was racing, I really didn't have a choice.

The crowd was impressive. Most of the women at the retreat had come out despite the gloomy weather, and it took me a while to realize that they weren't all racing. I glanced around anxiously for Allison. She had been out of my sight too long. I was still looking when Billie tapped me on the shoulder.

"I'm glad to see you both in one piece this morning," she whispered.

"Have you seen Allison?"

"She's getting her vest. They already called your name. Come on." As we walked, Billie explained the set-up. "There'll be another heat tomorrow," she said. "Half of us race today, half tomorrow, and then on Saturday there'll be a showdown between the top three racers from each day. The winner gets the whole week paid for!"

"But not everyone's racing?" I noticed that only twenty or so women were wearing the little vests being handed out.

"It's the first fifty to sign up. They've only got twenty-five sailboats, so it's limited. Good thing Allison signed us all up when she got here, huh?"

"The whole group from Women On Top is racing today?"

"Yes," she whispered. "Which means whoever's trying to kill Allison will be here too. I tried to talk her out of racing today, but she wouldn't even listen. She's not in a very good mood today. Is everything okay with you two?"

I managed a feeble smile. "Terrific."

Billie raised an eyebrow, but when I didn't elaborate, she shrugged. "Come on, let's find out what your emblem is." Billie's vest was orange and had a unicorn on the front. She put her arm around me and steered me toward the steps leading up to the lodge, where Buddy, still wearing his cowboy hat, was calling out names and Stella handed out vests.

Fay Daniels walked past in a vest adorned with a raccoon. "They've called your name twice," she said over her shoulder. Allison walked up behind us and fell in step. Her vest had intertwining hearts on the back and I couldn't help smiling at the irony. When I tried to catch her eye, she looked away.

"Cassidy James. Last call for Cassidy James!" I waved my hand at Buddy, and Stella handed me an orange vest with a butterfly across the back.

"Good luck!" Buddy said, winking at me. I waved again, and headed toward the starting line with Allison and Billie.

"What have you been up to?" Billie asked. "We were getting worried, weren't we, Allison?" Allison looked off toward the lake as if she were suddenly interested in the view.

"I was doing rule-outs," I said. "And making an ass of myself." I fingered the four remaining names in my pocket and looked around. Karen and Reeva were at the start of the line, talking to two young women wearing bathing suits and sneakers. They must be freezing, I thought. Or maybe I was just getting old. Even Reeva was only wearing a body shirt tucked into jeans. I stuck my hands into my jacket pockets and looked around until I finally spotted Sabrina sitting on a rock, waiting pensively for the race to begin.

"Here comes Holly," Billie said.

Sure enough, Lacy and Holly were making their way to the starting line. Lacy was her usual exuberant self and Holly was lagging behind. But I noticed something different about her, and it took me a minute to figure out what it was. Her smirk wasn't gone, but it didn't have the same degree of superiority it usually had. She wasn't smiling, and I couldn't say she looked radiant, or even happy, but somehow, without the full-on smirk, her whole face seemed to relax into something softer and more likeable. A kinder, gentler Holly, I thought, smiling.

Buddy had taken up a megaphone and was shouting directions into it like a cheerleader. The group immediately fell silent.

"First off, you gotta keep your vest on the whole time. You lose it, you're outta the race and you gotta pay for it. 'Cause Stella here made them herself and she don't want to make no more." This was met with chuckles. "Second, you gotta find the boat with the sails that match the vest. You take someone else's boat, you're automatically disqualified, and they have the right to take your boat instead. Third, if you lose a boat, it'll cost you whatever it takes to fix it. So don't go leaping out onto the island before you've pulled the boat safely ashore."

He paused, hitched up his jeans, then went on. "Okay. Once you get to the island, and after you've secured the boat, you gotta find the flag with your emblem on it. Now I know some of you are gonna complain that yours was harder to find than someone else's, but that's just the luck of the draw. They're all in plain sight and easy to find if you know where to look. Under no circumstances are you to touch someone else's flag. If you're caught doing that, and someone reports it, you'll be disqualified. Once you got your flag, it's smooth sailing back to this side. But you gotta dock your boat properly before you take off running. There'll be someone at the pier watching to make sure your vests match your sails, so don't even think about just leaping out and taking off. You gotta tie 'em up." He took a breath. "Finally, you ain't finished till you cross the finish line, right back here, with your flag in hand, and it better match your vest. Any questions?"

"Is there a prize for last place?" someone asked. People chuckled and Buddy rolled his eyes.

"Well, looking at the sky, I'd say whoever's last is likely to come in a might bit wet. You ladies ready?"

People moved up to the starting line and all talking stopped. Despite myself, I felt a familiar sensation in the pit of my stomach, and I realized, somewhat embarrassed, that I had butterflies. Just like in high school before a track meet, I thought. Only this time I wasn't competing for any medal. I was trying to keep Allison Crane, and maybe myself, alive.

The gun sounded, and more than a few women shrieked. We'd been expecting the pop of a starter pistol, but Buddy had fired a real gun into the air. Good way to get the old heart pumping, I thought, taking off with the others.

It didn't take long for the runners to separate themselves into groups according to speed. Billie and Sabrina were in the front with about four others, and it took every ounce of self-discipline I had not to charge up there alongside them. My competitive nature was almost getting the best of me. But Allison was a decent runner, and we were in the second group, not far behind the frontrunners. After that, the field dropped off, and when I turned around I could make out Karen and Holly in the group behind us, but there was no sign of Reeva, Fay or Lacy.

"You can go on ahead," Allison said. She still hadn't graced me with a look yet.

"If it's all the same to you, I'd rather stay where I am." The truth was, I was sore as hell and even running at this speed, I was hurting.

"Suit yourself." She was clearly mortified about what had happened last night, but what could I do? I was mortified myself.

"I think I just ruled out Holly," I said.

"Bully for you." She picked up speed. She had long legs and took graceful strides.

I'd always been a sprinter, and it was hard to pace myself beside her, especially after the ordeal in the water the day before. I tried to match her rhythm, but doing so reminded me of the night before, and I nearly tripped. I wasn't sure, but I thought a smile might have crossed her lips.

"You know how to sail?" she asked. At least she was starting to talk to me.

"I've done a little. I mean I know what the mainsail and the jib are. I know the difference between jibing and coming about. Sort of. To tell you the truth, it's been a while."

"There's no jib on these little boats. You've got one sail, and if you forget the difference between coming about and jibing, you're likely to get knocked out of the boat by the boom."

"That thingie the sail's attached to?" I asked, trying to make her smile.

"What's the matter? Don't they have sailboats on that lake of yours?"

"They've got them," I said. "I just don't happen to own one." We were coming up to the pier, and Allison was starting to breathe heavily. So was I, but I was doing my best to hide it.

"Okay, so tell me. What exactly is the difference between jibing and coming about?"

She looked at me, finally, and smiled. "You'll figure it out." Then, with a burst of speed I didn't know she still had, she surged ahead of me, sprinted down the length of the pier and leaped into a boat. I was still looking for the butterfly when the intertwined hearts flapped in the wind, caught it, and Allison sailed off without me. So much for protecting her, I thought. I'd be lucky if I was even able to catch up.

Chapter Twenty

My boat had a small basin and a slightly rounded V-hull. There was a single sail attached to a movable boom and it didn't take me long to remember how the "boom" had gotten its name. Every time I moved the tiller in an attempt to point the little boat in the right direction, the damn thing came swinging around, threatening to knock me into the water. By the time I got the hang of it, most of the other boats were well underway. Finally, the wind picked up and

I was able to catch a gust and start making some headway.

I wasn't the only one having trouble maneuvering her boat. In fact, if I hadn't been so intent on catching up to Allison, I'd have gotten a kick out of the yelps and curses scattered across the lake. Even though the island was directly across from the pier, not more than a couple of miles away, the boats were scattered far and wide. In a motorboat, it would've been a straight shot. But tacking back and forth while fighting the swirling gusts that changed direction without warning was indeed a formidable challenge. The boats that had gotten off early seemed to be faring much better. Those of us with a late start were struggling with the sudden shifts in the wind.

I tried to keep my eye on Allison's boat, but there was so much movement back and forth that I kept losing her. "Come on, Cassidy," I chastised myself. "You live on a lake, for God's sake. How hard can this be?" I hunkered down, squeezing the tiller between my arm and body, and pulled the sails tighter. This was called trimming the sails, I remembered. Well, if I trimmed them anymore, I'd be in the water. As it was, the little boat was heeled and I was slicing through the water at an alarming clip.

The island was egg-shaped, its highest point in the very center, with white sandy beaches exposed along its banks. In the spring and winter when the lake was higher, these beaches would be underwater, but at this time of year they provided nice moorings.

I'd imagined that there would be one particular spot where all the boats would pull up, but as I got closer to the island, I saw that the boats were scattered along the shore wherever someone could manage to land.

The wind was less fierce closer in and I cruised the shore, scanning the sails that flapped above the boats on the sandy beach. When I finally spotted the intertwined hearts, I headed straight in. Once I'd gotten the hang of it, I decided sailing was more fun than I'd remembered.

Allison's boat was off by itself, but she was nowhere in sight. *Terrific, Allison,* I thought. *You hire me to protect you, and then you get your feelings hurt and ditch me.*

I pulled my little boat up onto the bank beside hers and studied the sand for footprints. She'd headed straight up the bank and into the thick stand of cedar and fir trees that crowded the tiny island. I followed her footprints until they disappeared.

"Follow your instincts," I told myself. "Just pretend you're Allison and do what she'd do." I looked around and took a deep breath. Then I headed east.

The first flag I found bore a bumblebee emblem and was stuck between two branches of a pine. I passed it by, thinking that if it weren't for the fact that someone was trying to kill Allison, this race would be something I'd enjoy. The person who'd really enjoy it was Maggie. Maybe next year we'd come up here together, I thought, searching the forest for signs of my client.

I could hear the rustling of leaves and the crunching of twigs as women scoured the forest in search of their flags. Occasionally, a triumphant yelp could be heard, and I knew someone had found theirs.

Suddenly, a branch snapped right in front of me. "God, you scared me!" someone cried. It was one of the bathing suit-clad women that Reeva had been ogling earlier, and we'd nearly collided coming around a tree at the same time from opposite directions. "Have you seen a frog on a toadstool?" she asked, still holding her hand to her heart.

"Not back that way. So far, I've only seen a bumblebee."

"Oh, well. Say, I just saw a butterfly like you're wearing right back there. Through those trees and to the left."

"Thanks," I said. "Have you, by any chance, seen Allison Crane?"

"Nope. But if I see her, I'll tell her you were looking for her. See ya." She veered off to the right and disappeared into the forest.

I went toward the spot where she'd seen my flag. Sure enough, lodged between two rocks was a pointy-ended wooden pole with a flag that matched my emblem. I retrieved it and continued my search.

Overhead, the sky rumbled, a low angry growl that shook the ground. Seconds later, a fat raindrop plunked me on the head. Others fell, hitting the trees around me, and then it started to rain in earnest.

"It's raining!" I heard voices yell in the distance.

"Let's go back!" another voice shouted.

I joined the chorus of voices, calling Allison's name. I waited, then called again. There was no response. I'd hiked up to what seemed the center of the island, and from where I stood, I could see half a dozen participants scurrying toward the beach, none of whom I knew. The victorious shouts I'd heard each time someone located her flag grew more and more infrequent, and I decided to head back toward the boats. Most likely, Allison had found her flag and was already halfway back to the pier by now. I wasn't looking forward to sailing back in the rain, but from the look of the sky, it wasn't going to get any better. The sooner I got back, the better.

I retraced my steps as best I could, not sure I was going the exact same way I'd come but confident I was headed in the general direction. Several times I called Allison's name, but there was no answer. When I reached what I thought was the spot I'd left the boat, I stood under the protection of the trees and stared at the beach. Even through the rain, I could see the footprints, and there seemed to be more than there had been before. But to my dismay, there weren't any boats on the sand.

I looked out across the lake toward the resort and saw dozens of sailboats battling the choppy water. I tried to count them but lost track. It was impossible to make out the emblems on the sails in the driving rain. I had no way of knowing if Allison's boat was among them.

Perhaps I'd come back to the wrong spot, I thought. I pulled my windbreaker around me, wishing it were waterproof, and hopped down onto the beach. I stomped the sand and studied my shoeprint, comparing it to the ones already there. I was almost positive this was the same spot where we'd landed. There were drag marks in the sand from the boats.

One set of footprints led north along the edge of the water and I followed them.

"Allison!" I called. I wasn't at all sure the footsteps were hers, but I called out anyway.

When I saw her, my heart lurched. She was doubled over, clutching her side. She looked up, dazed, and fell to her knees in the sand. Her hair was soaked, and water streamed down her face. I ran as fast as I could.

"What happened?" I shouted. Then I noticed the blood. It had stained her jogging suit, a widening circle spreading across the left side of her ribcage.

"Somebody stabbed me." Her voice was a whisper and she was in obvious pain. "Just now, when you called out. They ran up there." She pointed to the forest behind us, and I scanned the area for movement, but saw nothing.

"Let me look." I lifted her sweatsuit jacket gingerly and she grimaced.

Her voice was strained. "I don't think they hit anything critical. But they might have gotten a rib. It hurts like hell." The wound was an ugly slash and had gone fairly deep. The blood seeped out in a steady flow.

"Can you reach your right arm around here to hold this?" I asked. I ripped the butterfly flag off of its wooden pole and folded it into squares until I had a thick bandage. I pressed it against the wound. She nodded, grunting with the effort. There was sweat mixing with the rain on her brow.

"They took the boats," she whispered. She pointed north, away from the resort and for the first time, I noticed the two boats, sails flapping listlessly as they bobbed on the water a hundred feet from shore. The wind was taking them farther away from the island. "We're stranded," she said.

"Did you see who it was?" I looked back toward the forest, wondering if the attacker was watching us now.

"She just jumped me. Once I saw the boats, I sat down on the bank to think. I didn't know if you were still on the island, and I wasn't sure what to do. I didn't even hear her come up behind me. The first thing I heard was a grunt, and I started to turn, but the knife was already in my ribs. And then you called my name, and she just disappeared before I could even look up."

"Can you walk?"

"Not very far. With stab wounds, it's best if you stay quiet and try to staunch the bleeding. I don't think she punctured any organs, but there's no point in bleeding to death."

I nodded. She was right, of course. I reached into my jacket and pulled out my thirty-eight, setting it on the ground in front of her.

"If anyone comes, use this. Turn around so you can face the forest, so you can see them coming."

"Where are you going?" she asked, her eyes huge. She touched the gun with her index finger and quickly pulled it back. She reminded me of a curious kid who touches a snake's skin for the first time.

"I'm going after them," I said. "I'm getting tired of being hunted. It's time to turn the tables."

"Cassidy," she reached out and took hold of my arm. "I'm afraid." Her blue-green eyes searched my face.

"You'll be okay," I said. "Have you ever fired one

of these?" I picked up the gun and showed her how. She watched me and nodded.

"I'm afraid for *you*," she said. I didn't know if the tears were from pain or emotion.

"I'll be okay. But I do need to get going."

"I'm sorry about last night," she said, letting the tears fall.

"Shhh . . ." I brushed the tears off her cheek and leaned forward, doing something that surprised me even as I did it. I cupped her lovely face and kissed her softly on the lips. It was excruciatingly tender. It lasted only a few seconds, but it seemed longer.

"I could have loved you," she said, looking into my eyes.

"I know," I said. I stood up, my legs shaking. "I could have loved you, too."

I leaped up onto the grassy ledge above the beach and ran into the forest, my heart pounding, my throat tight with emotion, the wooden flagpole with its pointed end still clutched in my hand like a spear.

Chapter Twenty-one

I'd have liked it better if I'd known which suspect I was chasing. It might make a difference in how they tried to trap me, which was what I was anticipating. But I didn't have that luxury, so I just forged ahead.

As quickly as possible, I leapt from rock to rock, avoiding the twigs along the forest floor. I stopped often, listening, but the sound of the rain overhead drowned out most other noises. That was good. They'd have trouble hearing me, too. As I ran, I scanned the ground, looking for footprints, anything that might indicate a direction. I knew, though, that with all the women who'd been here in the last hour, footprints probably wouldn't be much help. Even so, when I found some heading east, I followed them.

I was nearly to the highest part of the island when I heard a crashing sound ahead of me. I stopped, my heart thudding against my chest. Slowly, I crept forward toward the noise, wishing I had my gun.

Just then, a flash of color caught my eye through the thick foliage, not fifty feet away. It was gone as quickly as it appeared, a yellow blur between the trees, but it had been enough. What I'd seen was the unmistakable silhouette of Reeva's flattop.

Of course, I thought. Reeva was the one with the Swiss Army knife. I wished I had something more than just the skinny flag pole in my hand. Still, clutching it made me feel somewhat better, and I stealthily made my way after her disappearing form.

She was much more quick and lithe than I would've given her credit for. Like a feral cat, she moved from rock to rock, much as I'd been doing. I followed her, staying back, wondering what she was up to. She seemed to be circling back toward the spot where I'd left Allison. Judging from the way she moved, it was almost as if she were hunting something. But I was behind her. Did she know I was following her? Was this some kind of elaborate trap? I stayed low and did my best to keep up with her, waiting for the break I would need in order to make a move.

It came so suddenly I almost missed it. We'd been traveling downhill, back toward the lakeshore, and the path she was following wound through the trees in a spiral. When I saw her, she was crouched on a flat rock, watching the forest in front of her, almost directly below me. I, too, was crouched on a rock, and when I realized I'd finally gotten my chance, my heartbeat quickened.

As quietly as I could, I stood up, counted to three and heaved myself off the rock, landing directly on top of her. She let out a terrifying yell and rolled over, taking me with her.

"You!" she panted, grabbing me by the hair and slamming me to the ground. She was bigger and stronger than I was, and she was wild with rage.

"Give it up, Reeva," I managed. I still clutched the pole in my right hand, but she was too close for me to use it. I dropped it and punched my fist into her throat. She let go of me, clutching her neck. I knew this might be the only break I got. With all the strength my legs could muster, I kicked her, connecting with her chin. She went flying backwards. But before I could get to my feet, she was on hers. The red army knife was in her hand.

"You don't understand," she said, circling me. Her eyes were wild, and blood trickled down the corner of her mouth where I'd kicked her.

"You're jealous of Allison," I said. "Everyone loves her and you wish they loved you. You've got great ideas, but no one will listen. How's that, Reeva? Close enough?"

She was shaking her head and her eyes kept darting around as if she expected the cops to arrive at any moment. She had a wild-eyed look that scared me. "It's not me," she said, panting.

"No? You've got some alter ego doing all this? Put down the knife, Reeva. There's been enough damage done." I was breathing heavily myself, tired of circling. But she wouldn't stop.

"I don't hate Allison," she said, huffing noisily. "One of *them* does." Her eyes had gone steely and were fixed on something over my left shoulder. Hearing a twig snap behind me, I wheeled around.

Sabrina Pepper and Fay Daniels stood facing each other in the pounding rain, both looking wild-eyed with fear. Sabrina clutched a bloody knife which she waved at Fay.

"She tried to kill Allison! I saw her!" Sabrina wailed.

Fay took a tentative step backwards, holding her hands in front of her. "Cut the act, Sabrina, and put down the knife before you hurt someone else." She looked at Reeva and me for help. "I saw her running out of the woods and followed her. I just hope to God Allison's okay."

"She's lying!" Sabrina shouted. "I didn't do it! She did!"

Reeva and I exchanged glances, not knowing what to believe. Cautiously, the two of us moved in closer, flanking them.

"What were you doing out here?" I asked Fay.

"Following her! Obviously she's the one who's been trying to kill Allison. When I saw her with the knife, I knew I had to stop her."

"That's not true! It was you! You tried to hide the knife and I found it! Reeva, you know I wouldn't hurt Allison!"

"Which one were you following?" I asked Reeva.

"Sabrina," she said. "When it started to rain, I headed back to the boat and that's when I saw her run by with the knife."

The four of us stood in the downpour, looking from one to the other. We were streaked with mud, the hair plastered to our heads.

I finally broke the silence and turned to Fay. "If you were following Sabrina, how did she get behind you?"

Fay's eyes narrowed. She took a tentative step toward Sabrina, her hand held in front of her. "Give me the knife, Sabrina." Her gray Army T-shirt was soaked through and I recognized it from her room as the one with the name penned on the label. The name Anderson. Suddenly, I felt a chill run through me. The connection I'd been searching for was right in front of me.

"Put down the knife, Sabrina," I said, moving closer. Sabrina's eyes worried me. They were glassy with false bravado. She clutched the knife even tighter, not taking her eyes from Fay.

"Tell me, Fay. Did you used to have a sister? A younger one, perhaps?" I took another step toward her, keeping an eye on Sabrina's knife. Fay shot me a quick glance, then turned her attention back to Sabrina. "I know you're married, Fay. Your maiden name was Anderson, right? It says so on your shirt label. And your sister was Mary Ann. Only they called her Andy. She was Allison's first lover, wasn't she?" This time, Fay's attention was riveted on me. Her lips had gone into a snarl. "She killed herself and you blamed Allison," I finished, taking another step toward her.

"I don't know what you're talking about," she spat.

"It's a long time to hold a grudge, Fay. Did it

take you all this time to track Allison down, or just this long to get up the courage to try to kill her?"

"You're as crazy as she is! I didn't try to kill anyone. Look at her! She's the one who's disturbed!"

Reeva took another step toward Sabrina and held out her hand. "Give me the knife, babe. No one's going to hurt you."

"She tried to pin the murder on you, Reeva! Don't you see? All those notes about football? She was trying to frame you and now she's doing the same to me!" Sabrina's pupils had become pinpoints, tiny dots of black disappearing into vapid pools of blue. She stared at Fay, hatred seeping from every pore. Suddenly, she lunged.

"No!" Reeva and I shouted together. Before we could stop her, Sabrina was on top of Fay, pummeling her with her fists, the bloody knife still lying on the ground where she had dropped it.

As strong as she was, Fay was no match for Sabrina's fury. By the time Reeva and I managed to pull Sabrina away, Fay was nearly unconscious. Sabrina collapsed on the ground, a thin smile spreading across her pale complexion.

"Touchdown!" she whispered, blowing blond bangs off her forehead. Then she fainted.

We made quite a motley crew. Reeva carried Sabrina all the way back to the beach and I helped Fay hobble behind them. She offered no resistance. She seemed broken, as if all the life had gone out of her.

We now sat beside Allison, waiting for someone to notice our absence. The rain had let up and there was even a thread of sunshine stretching through the clouds. Sabrina had regained consciousness and seemed a different person — stronger somehow, and more at peace with herself. She was curled up with her head on Reeva's shoulder, a strange smile playing at the corners of her mouth.

Allison seemed to have gone into shock, not from the knife wound, but from the news that Fay was Andy's sister. The old pain of her lover's suicide was made new by the realization that someone besides herself had blamed her for the death. Fay refused to look at any of us, refused to speak or to explain her actions. She sat stoically, staring out at the lake, her bloodied nose dripping onto the front of her T-shirt. When I tried to stem the flow, she turned her head, refusing even that small gesture.

Reeva and I took turns consoling Allison, but finally we just let her cry. I held one hand and Reeva held the other, lending her our strength while she finally let go of years of silent grief.

"I've made so many mistakes," Allison said, when she'd finally cried herself out. Fay snorted, a pathetic sound, given her bloodied nose. She quickly resumed her silence.

Reeva put her arm around Allison. "We all have, babe. No one's perfect. Even you. Though you're about as close as they come. To tell you the truth, I like you better knowing you're mortal." Reeva reached over and punched me playfully in the arm. "What about you, cowgirl? You ever do anything wrong?"

"I was wrong about you," I admitted. "When I saw you up there in the woods, I thought —"

"No shit, Sherlock. I've damn near got a broken chin to prove it. But that's not what I meant." She let it hang, and so did I.

Allison couldn't stand it. "What?"

"She wants to know if I'm really John Girl in disguise. I think she wants to know if we slept together."

Allison's cheeks turned slightly pink, but she covered quickly. "Are you kidding? Cassidy James is madly in love with some woman named Maggie, and she wouldn't even think of screwing that up. In fact, rumor has it, they're about to have their one-year anniversary. Am I right?" She poked me in the ribs. Obviously, Billie had told all.

"Absolutely," I said, feeling both proud and achingly sad.

"Well, you sure did a good job of acting, I'll give you that," Reeva said. In the distance, an aluminum motorboat chugged toward us, battling the waves.

Allison snuck her hand over and squeezed mine. I squeezed back. The electricity that passed between us could've lit a city.

Chapter Twenty-two

It was the first citizen's arrest I'd ever made,
and hopefully the last. Once the police finally arrived,
I was almost sorry I'd contacted them. There was no
end to the depositions and statements. The fact that
Fay had maintained her vow of silence, refusing to
speak, or even to eat or drink, didn't help matters.
Fay's estranged husband had been summoned and
was finally able to shed some light on the situation.
He was a timid man, as nervous as he was concerned.

"She saw Allison Crane's name in the paper," he explained, "and it ate away at her. Back when the suicide happened, she believed it had been her sister who was twisted. Allison claimed to be straight and so no one really blamed her. But then, here she turns out to be the president of some damned homosexual group and flaunting it like she's proud of it, and it was more than Fay could bear. I tried to tell her the past was the past, but she became obsessed. When she told me she wanted to spend some time away from me on her own, I thought maybe she had met another man. Then the next thing I know, she's quit the Army and run off to Portland. Things weren't that good between us anyway, but when she wouldn't return my calls, I got worried. I never thought it would come to this, though. Never in a million years."

Martha came up and helped cut through the red tape. Even with Fay's husband's testimony, the local police seemed overwhelmed by the twists and turns. Finally, they decided to take Fay back to town for questioning. By then, it was Sunday, the day before everyone's scheduled departure.

Meanwhile, Martha was in her true element. An attractive cop with a Don Juan complex and a romantic history that made mine look anemic, Martha positively glowed. Women have always swarmed to Martha. She exudes this kind of sexuality that few straight people would understand. But I knew she had Tina at home. I also knew that Tina was the first woman Martha had ever really committed herself to, and that they had something special. I wasn't about to let her screw that up.

"Maybe we should wait until everyone pulls out," she said, flashing me those big brown eyes of hers that had melted my own heart once, long ago.

"We're going now, Martha."

Reluctantly, she agreed to accompany me down the mountain.

"I suppose you'll be wanting Diablo," Buddy said. His grin was ear to ear. I'd gained status now that he knew I was a private investigator, and he'd been bird-dogging me.

"Absolutely," I said. "Unless you want him?" I glanced at Martha. She looked unsure. Until she saw Diablo. His eyes were all whites rolled back in his head and he pawed the ground, snorting.

"No thanks. I'll stick with Sugar Babe."

Buddy and I laughed.

"You won't be a stranger, now," Billie said, clicking her fancy camera in my direction. She was wearing the same white outfit I'd seen her in the first day, which seemed like a year ago. She was a truly lovely person, I thought, and again I was struck with the notion that she was on the wrong end of the camera. I flashed her a smile and hoped the camera would reveal how I felt.

"Even Diablo couldn't keep me away," I said. I looked at Allison and couldn't quite hold the smile. We'd hardly talked since first the police and then Martha and Fay's husband had arrived. Things had happened so fast, I thought. And there'd been too much to say and too little time to say it.

"The check's in the mail," she said.

"You already paid me, Allie."

She took my hands, pulled me close. "You'll see."
She leaned forward and whispered in my ear, "Thank
you."

I looked at her blankly.

"For Billie."

I looked into her eyes, looked at Billie and smiled.
Billie was beaming. "Don't thank me," I said. "Billie's
the one who's put up with you all this time. Con-
gratulations."

She hugged me good-bye, a good, innocent hug
that lasted only a second longer than absolutely
necessary. I swung up onto Diablo, who immediately
laid his ears back, and I clicked my tongue, urging
him forward.

"Ride 'em cowgirl!" I turned in time to see Karen
tip her baseball cap in my direction. She had her
arm around Sabrina, a lopsided grin on her face.
Sabrina just smiled, and Reeva, standing next to
them, shot me a thumbs up.

Lacy, looking as much like Shirley Temple as ever,
was rocking on her heels, waving enthusiastically. I
waved back, even at Holly who was off in a corner
pretending to study the fence. I thought I caught a
real smile, but I wasn't sure. It may have been a
smirk.

"Didn't take you long to make friends," Martha
said. She was on a big dun mare who plodded along
the trail like a somnambulant cow.

"It's not making friends that's hard," I said,
feeling ridiculously philosophical. "It's keeping them."

"Well, you've managed to keep me all these years.
You can't be all bad."

"Face it, Harper. You're easy."

"With women, maybe. Not with friends." I knew this was true, and let it drop.

The really great thing about best friends is you don't have to talk. We rode down the mountain behind Buddy in companionable silence. I listened to the waterfalls recede, and the smell of sulphur, which I'd grown used to, slowly dissipated. I could picture the lake getting smaller and smaller behind me. I felt the tiny cabins disappear into the past. I imagined Allison's smile, her touch, her laughing eyes, and knew I'd carry them with me no matter how distant the memory became. And I thought of Fay, carrying a sadness with her all these years until it turned to rage and became the sole focus of her life. Then I saw Sabrina blowing blond bangs off her forehead, an unlikely warrior scoring the final point. Finally, opening my eyes to the bright sunshine around me, I nudged Diablo with my heels and challenged Martha to a race across the last meadow leading to T-Bone Ranch.

Chapter Twenty-three

The brief series of storms had passed and the sun beat down on my dock as if summer had never been interrupted. Maggie was trying out a fly rod we'd bought at a garage sale. Luckily there was no hook attached, because Panic and Gammon leaped at every backcast she made, more often than not catching the tiny fly before she had a chance to whip it into the water.

"Looks like you're getting the hang of it," I said, honestly glad to be back home. I sat down on the warm dock and pulled Gammon onto my lap.

Maggie grimaced, then cast again. She wasn't really speaking to me yet. I'd gotten home late Sunday, and hadn't seen her until this morning. I'd missed our anniversary. Worse, with everything that had happened, I hadn't had time to do anything about her present. She brought my present with her. That's when I realized I'd screwed up.

"Open it," she said. "You may as well."

"Maggie."

"It's okay, Cass. I know you've been under a lot of pressure. I know there were no stores up there with all those naked lesbians walking around. I understand."

I sighed. "Maggie, what makes you think there were naked lesbians walking around?"

"Weren't there?"

To my utter dismay, I blushed.

"That's what I thought," she said, whipping the line into the water.

"Maggie, I didn't forget. Honest. It's just . . ."

"Cass, it's okay. I'm not mad. Really." She set the rod down on the dock and came over. She was wearing a ridiculously sexy blouse tucked into cutoffs. Her legs were long and tan, her green eyes as captivating as ever. My heart did a little skip when she took my hands.

"I just missed you," she said.

"I missed you too."

"Even with all those women fawning all over you?"

"Nobody fawned," I assured her.

"Not even that presidential doctor? The one with the red hair? The one you shared a room with while you were posing as her girlfriend?"

I sighed. I sighed again. I tried not to blush.

"She did, didn't she? Shit! She fawned over you! I can't believe it!"

"She didn't fawn," I said.

"What then? Something happened. I can tell!"

"Maggie, nothing happened. Okay? Nothing. She hired me. I did my job. In the process we became friends. That's it."

She picked up the present she'd brought. It was large and flat, and looked suspiciously like a picture. It was wrapped in red paper. I was afraid she might throw it into the water.

"How good of friends?" she asked.

I thought about it, thought about how to answer. "Very," I said. "We became very good friends." I looked her in the eye. I held the gaze. I did not blush. I didn't need to.

"I made the frame," she said finally. "Rick did the rest."

"He did? He's painting again?" My eyes teary, I carefully ripped open the package. I couldn't believe what I saw. "That's us!" I said, dumbfounded. "Oh, Maggie, it's beautiful!"

"It was his idea." She was clearly as moved as I was. The painting showed two women, one with black glossy curls and sea-green eyes, the other a laughing blonde. They were running hand in hand through a field of wildflowers. To me, it was the best painting Rick had ever done.

We were still gazing at it when we heard the sound of an approaching boat.

"Isn't that Tommy?" she asked.

Sure enough, Tommy Greene, the marina attendant, was coming toward us at putt-putt speed. It was so unusual to see him going slowly, that we both stood and watched.

"What's that he's got behind him?" Maggie asked. It looked like he was towing something. And he was heading straight for our dock.

"Have to wait and see," I said. Frankly, I had no idea. I carefully set the picture in the cabin of my Sea Swirl and went back to stand beside Maggie.

"Looks like a sailboat," she said. It did. And no sooner had she said it than I recognized the emblem on the sail, flapping benevolently in the breeze behind Tommy's boat.

" 'Afternoon, ladies," Tommy shouted. His sunburned, elfin face was grinning from ear to pointy ear.

" 'Afternoon, Tommy." My throat had constricted and I felt my face grow warm.

"Understand there's cause to celebrate!"

Maggie looked at me questioningly. I shrugged. What else could I do?

"They said this was a rush order, so I brought it right out. Guess I'll let you two get back to, well, whatever it is you were doing." He turned away, and quickly tied the sailboat to a metal cleat on the dock. He hopped back into his boat and roared away, leaving the little boat to rock against the dock.

"You didn't forget," Maggie said, hugging me to her. "God, it's just perfect! How'd you know I've been dying for a sailboat? Come on, hop in!"

Even though it was barely big enough for the two of us, I got in, looking up at the single sail luffing in the breeze. She was right, it was perfect. The two hearts, intertwined, seemed to glow with the sun behind them.

I lay my head on Maggie's leg, letting her guide the boat, watching the wind catch the sail, feeling ridiculously happy. Sometimes, I thought, the greatest gifts really are surprises.

Epilogue

In September I was summoned to Portland to testify in Fay Daniels' trial but on the day I was to appear, the case was settled. Fay's attorney had plea bargained with the prosecution, and even Allison supported the decision that Fay spend time getting help rather than in prison. The judge placed Fay on probation for five years, provided a portion of that time be spent in Veteran's Hospital in Seattle where she was to undergo psychiatric treatment. She was still there when I visited almost a year later.

I came unannounced, but it was clear that Fay

had been expecting someone. She was waiting in the visiting lounge and when I entered her face lit up momentarily before she realized who I was.

"Oh! I thought you were someone else," she said. We stood staring at each other for a long moment until finally she regained her composure. "Come on in." She ushered me to the far corner, away from the television set and the few other people in the room. I sat on a plastic chair and marveled at how she'd changed. Her once-long ponytail was gone and her hair was now nearly as short as Reeva's. Somehow, the change suited her. It was almost as if, free of the ponytail, she had become younger, more at-ease with herself. She was wearing a bright orange turtleneck that accentuated her ample physique and I wondered what had happened to all those oversized, gray sweatshirts.

"You want some coffee?" She walked to a table set up with an aluminum dispenser and a stack of Styrofoam cups. Not waiting for an answer, she poured black liquid into two cups, and came to sit across from me.

I took a tentative sip, remembering her propensity for poisoning people, and her eyes met mine. "You want to know why I did it, I suppose." She sat back against her chair and took a dainty sip from her cup.

"Actually, I wanted to know how you were," I said. She appraised me coolly. I sighed. "Okay, I also want to understand why you did it."

She laughed aloud and seemed to relax a little. "Go ahead and drink your coffee, Cass. No poison, honest! It's decaf."

"Your husband explained quite a bit," I said, embarrassed that she'd read me so easily. "When Andy died, you had no one to blame but her for taking her own life. To all appearances, Allison was straight. Then, all these years later when you discovered Allison was not only gay, but the president of a successful lesbian organization, you —"

"Go ahead and say it. I lost it. And all that's true, to an extent. But what my well-meaning husband didn't understand, is that I never really did blame Andy." She looked up at the ceiling as if gathering resolve. "I blamed myself." She took another drink and leveled her gaze at me. "It's taken a lot of work for me to finally be able to say this. I, too, had feelings for girls, though God knows I never admitted it, even to myself." She looked at me, waiting for some reaction. I returned her gaze and waited. "When Andy killed herself, I thought that somehow her infatuation with Allison was my fault. That somehow my own secret perversion had rubbed off on her."

The TV blared suddenly, causing me to start. "But how did you get from blaming yourself to blaming Allison, and from there, to wanting to kill her?"

"That's one of the things I've been working on in therapy. You have to understand that until recently, I didn't realize that I'd *been* blaming myself. Discovering Allison was one of life's little ironies. It gave me a focus for my bottled up anger. It's also what has allowed me to finally accept who I am." She paused, exhaling noisily. "The people at Women On Top were the first real family I'd had since Andy died. I hadn't expected to feel welcomed. I wanted to hate them all."

"But you didn't."

"How could I? They were everything Andy would've been. They were what I should have been all along." She got up to refill her coffee, seemingly embarrassed by this admission. There were so many things I wanted to ask her, but they seemed insignificant in light of what she'd just told me.

Again, Fay seemed to read my mind. "You probably wonder why I stuck you with a needle that day." She came to stand in front of me. "As I'm sure you know, I was an RN in the Army. Good at it, too. I probably know as much about dosages as Allison does. It wasn't difficult to get my hands on some Nitroglycerin. Truth is, I could've tried harder to kill you. For that matter, I could've tried harder to kill Allison." She took a breath, and went on. "My shrink says that the reason I never succeeded in killing anyone was because I didn't really want to. I don't know. At the time, I sure thought I did. When you started getting in the way, I had no choice but to come after you. If it's any consolation, I really did like you. Things just got out of hand, that's all."

This was probably the understatement of the year, but I decided not to press the issue.

"Tell me about the football notes," I said at last.

"You thought it was Reeva, didn't you? At first, I mean. I wasn't really trying to frame her, so much as make fun of her. I know it sounds crazy, but she was such an obvious culprit. Maybe I wasn't making fun of her as much as I was making fun of everyone else. You did just about fall for it, didn't you?"

I admitted that I had. "What about the pâte? And the cereal?"

"Cereal? You lost me."

I explained about Allison's cereal and Fay

frowned. "It was the milk. Damn, I didn't know about the cat." She stood again and started to pace. "I wondered what happened. It seemed like everything I tried backfired. Of course, I couldn't ask anyone. Half the time, I never knew what went wrong. Allison wasn't telling anyone anything, and I wasn't exactly thinking clearly."

She stopped suddenly and thrust her hands on her hips, gracing me with a crooked smile. "You almost caught me that night I was leaving the pâte in Allison's cabin. I think, subconsciously, I was hoping to get caught. I just didn't know it."

"What was in the pâte?" I asked. I'd always wondered.

"Oleander."

"No rat poison?"

"I hadn't thought of that," she said, giggling. Despite myself, I laughed. This woman was growing on me. "More coffee?" she asked. I looked at my empty cup and back at her calm gray eyes. Maybe it was I who was nuts. I handed her my cup.

"This is Andy," she said, taking a yellowing photo encased in plastic from her back pocket. "Sixteen and the whole world in front of her. God she was sweet."

"You don't look anything alike," I said. No wonder Allison hadn't recognized Fay.

"Isn't that the truth? You know what they called me in sixth grade? Art-fay. That's Pig Latin, of course. It carried over all the way into high school. I'm just glad I was out of there before Andy's freshman year. At least she didn't have my sorry face hanging over her through high school." She gazed fondly at the photo before returning it to her pocket. "Unlike me, she was very popular. Could've had any boy in school. Then Allison Crane came along." She took an exaggerated breath and rested her head against the wall. "I'm still not totally okay with this," she said, letting her breath out slowly. "But you'd be surprised how far I've come."

"It's obvious how far you've come, Fay. I think Andy would be proud."

"Yeah, well. The thing is, the big fucking ironic thing is, that if *I* had met an Allison Crane when *I* was sixteen, I would've never done this, and maybe Andy might still be alive. Where was I when she needed a big sister to tell her that what she was feeling was natural? I was such a loser, Cass. Andy ended up dead, but I was the loser. She had more guts than I ever did. I've never even kissed a woman."

"It's not too late, Fay."

She looked up, eyes wet and glossy. "I know. Actually, I think I've met someone. I hope. She comes in to visit her sister every week and we've struck up a friendship. I've told her everything. Even about Allison. She's a good listener and I think she likes me, too." She smiled a smile I'd seen before. It was the look of someone who has recently discovered the possibility of love. I finished my coffee, smiling myself, and got up to go.

Suddenly, the visitor's door opened again and Fay stood up, nervously smoothing her hair. I followed her gaze and saw the object of Fay's new-found desire. The woman was in her forties, with short dark hair and cheeks flushed pink with the cold. Clutched in her gloved hand was a single red rose. She beamed at Fay, then saw me and her smile froze. "Oh!" she said.

"I was just leaving. Fay and I are old friends."

"Oh." She seemed relieved, if a little doubtful.

"Cass is one of the ones I tried to kill," Fay blurted.

The woman looked from me to Fay with concern. "Oh. I see." She moved the rose to her other hand, unsure what to do. "You seem to have come through it all right," she said, finally. Even Fay laughed at this.

I turned to Fay and extended my hand. "Good luck," I said.

"Thank you. It means a lot that you came." She held onto my hand another moment, then turned to her visitor and accepted the proffered rose.

A few of the publications of
THE NAIAD PRESS, INC.
P.O. Box 10543   Tallahassee, Florida 32302
Phone (850) 539-5965
Toll-Free Order Number: 1-800-533-1973
Mail orders welcome. Please include 15% postage.
Write or call for our free catalog which also features an
incredible selection of lesbian videos.

FOURTH DOWN by Kate Calloway. 240 pp. 4th Cassidy James mystery. ISBN 1-56280-205-4 $11.95

A MOMENT'S INDISCRETION by Peggy J. Herring. 176 pp. There's a fine line between love and lust . . . ISBN 1-56280-194-5 11.95

CITY LIGHTS/COUNTRY CANDLES by Penny Hayes. 208 pp. About the women she has known . . . 11.95

POSSESSIONS by Kaye Davis. 240 pp. 2nd Maris Middleton mystery. ISBN 1-56280-192-9 11.95

A QUESTION OF LOVE by Saxon Bennett. 208 pp. Every woman is granted one great love. ISBN 1-56280-205-4 11.95

RHYTHM TIDE by Frankie J. Jones. 160 pp. . . . to desire passionately and be passionately desired. ISBN 1-56280-189-9 11.95

PENN VALLEY PHOENIX by Janet McClellan. 208 pp. 2nd Tru North Mystery. ISBN 1-56280-200-3 11.95

BY RESERVATION ONLY by Jackie Calhoun. 240 pp. A chance for true happiness. ISBN 1-56280-191-0 11.95

OLD BLACK MAGIC by Jaye Maiman. 272 pp. 9th Robin Miller mystery. ISBN 1-56280-175-9 11.95

LEGACY OF LOVE by Marianne K. Martin. 240 pp. Women will do anything for her . . . ISBN 1-56280-184-8 11.95

LETTING GO by Ann O'Leary. 160 pp. Laura, at 39, in love with 23-year-old Kate. ISBN 1-56280-183-X 11.95

LADY BE GOOD edited by Barbara Grier and Christine Cassidy. 288 pp. Erotic stories by Naiad Press authors. ISBN 1-56280-180-5 14.95

CHAIN LETTER by Claire McNab. 288 pp. 9th Carol Ashton mystery. ISBN 1-56280-181-3 11.95

NIGHT VISION by Laura Adams. 256 pp. Erotic fantasy romance by "famous" author. ISBN 1-56280-182-1 11.95

SEA TO SHINING SEA by Lisa Shapiro. 256 pp. Unable to resist the raging passion . . . ISBN 1-56280-177-5 11.95

THIRD DEGREE by Kate Calloway. 224 pp. 3rd Cassidy James mystery. ISBN 1-56280-185-6   11.95

WHEN THE DANCING STOPS by Therese Szymanski. 272 pp. 1st Brett Higgins mystery. ISBN 1-56280-186-4   11.95

PHASES OF THE MOON by Julia Watts. 192 pp. . . . . hungry for everything life has to offer. ISBN 1-56280-176-7   11.95

BABY IT'S COLD by Jaye Maiman. 256 pp. 5th Robin Miller mystery. ISBN 1-56280-156-2   10.95

CLASS REUNION by Linda Hill. 176 pp. The girl from her past . . . ISBN 1-56280-178-3   11.95

DREAM LOVER by Lyn Denison. 224 pp. A soft, sensuous, romantic fantasy. ISBN 1-56280-173-1   11.95

FORTY LOVE by Diana Simmonds. 288 pp. Joyous, heart-warming romance. ISBN 1-56280-171-6   11.95

IN THE MOOD by Robbi Sommers. 160 pp. The queen of erotic tension! ISBN 1-56280-172-4   11.95

SWIMMING CAT COVE by Lauren Douglas. 192 pp. 2nd Allison O'Neil Mystery. ISBN 1-56280-168-6   11.95

THE LOVING LESBIAN by Claire McNab and Sharon Gedan. 240 pp. Explore the experiences that make lesbian love unique. ISBN 1-56280-169-4   14.95

COURTED by Celia Cohen. 160 pp. Sparkling romantic encounter. ISBN 1-56280-166-X   11.95

SEASONS OF THE HEART by Jackie Calhoun. 240 pp. Romance through the years. ISBN 1-56280-167-8   11.95

K. C. BOMBER by Janet McClellan. 208 pp. 1st Tru North mystery. ISBN 1-56280-157-0   11.95

LAST RITES by Tracey Richardson. 192 pp. 1st Stevie Houston mystery. ISBN 1-56280-164-3   11.95

EMBRACE IN MOTION by Karin Kallmaker. 256 pp. A whirlwind love affair. ISBN 1-56280-165-1   11.95

HOT CHECK by Peggy J. Herring. 192 pp. Will workaholic Alice fall for guitarist Ricky? ISBN 1-56280-163-5   11.95

OLD TIES by Saxon Bennett. 176 pp. Can Cleo surrender to a passionate new love? ISBN 1-56280-159-7   11.95

LOVE ON THE LINE by Laura DeHart Young. 176 pp. Will Stef win Kay's heart? ISBN 1-56280-162-7   11.95

DEVIL'S LEG CROSSING by Kaye Davis. 192 pp. 1st Maris Middleton mystery. ISBN 1-56280-158-9   11.95

COSTA BRAVA by Marta Balletbo Coll. 144 pp. Read the book, see the movie! ISBN 1-56280-153-8   11.95

WILDWOOD FLOWERS by Julia Watts. 208 pp. Hilarious and heart-warming tale of true love. ISBN 1-56280-127-9   10.95

NEVER SAY NEVER by Linda Hill. 224 pp. Rule #1: Never get involved with . . . ISBN 1-56280-126-0   11.95

THE SEARCH by Melanie McAllester. 240 pp. Exciting top cop Tenny Mendoza case. ISBN 1-56280-150-3   10.95

THE WISH LIST by Saxon Bennett. 192 pp. Romance through the years. ISBN 1-56280-125-2   10.95

FIRST IMPRESSIONS by Kate Calloway. 208 pp. P.I. Cassidy James' first case. ISBN 1-56280-133-3   10.95

OUT OF THE NIGHT by Kris Bruyer. 192 pp. Spine-tingling thriller. ISBN 1-56280-120-1   10.95

NORTHERN BLUE by Tracey Richardson. 224 pp. Police recruits Miki & Miranda — passion in the line of fire. ISBN 1-56280-118-X   10.95

LOVE'S HARVEST by Peggy J. Herring. 176 pp. by the author of Once More With Feeling. ISBN 1-56280-117-1   10.95

THE COLOR OF WINTER by Lisa Shapiro. 208 pp. Romantic love beyond your wildest dreams. ISBN 1-56280-116-3   10.95

FAMILY SECRETS by Laura DeHart Young. 208 pp. Enthralling romance and suspense. ISBN 1-56280-119-8   10.95

INLAND PASSAGE by Jane Rule. 288 pp. Tales exploring conventional & unconventional relationships. ISBN 0-930044-56-8   10.95

DOUBLE BLUFF by Claire McNab. 208 pp. 7th Carol Ashton Mystery. ISBN 1-56280-096-5   10.95

BAR GIRLS by Lauran Hoffman. 176 pp. See the movie, read the book! ISBN 1-56280-115-5   10.95

THE FIRST TIME EVER edited by Barbara Grier & Christine Cassidy. 272 pp. Love stories by Naiad Press authors. ISBN 1-56280-086-8   14.95

MISS PETTIBONE AND MISS McGRAW by Brenda Weathers. 208 pp. A charming ghostly love story. ISBN 1-56280-151-1   10.95

CHANGES by Jackie Calhoun. 208 pp. Involved romance and relationships. ISBN 1-56280-083-3   10.95

FAIR PLAY by Rose Beecham. 256 pp. An Amanda Valentine Mystery. ISBN 1-56280-081-7   10.95

PAYBACK by Celia Cohen. 176 pp. A gripping thriller of romance, revenge and betrayal. ISBN 1-56280-084-1   10.95

THE BEACH AFFAIR by Barbara Johnson. 224 pp. Sizzling summer romance/mystery/intrigue. ISBN 1-56280-090-6   10.95

GETTING THERE by Robbi Sommers. 192 pp. Nobody does it like Robbi! ISBN 1-56280-099-X   10.95

FINAL CUT by Lisa Haddock. 208 pp. 2nd Carmen Ramirez Mystery.   ISBN 1-56280-088-4   10.95

FLASHPOINT by Katherine V. Forrest. 256 pp. A Lesbian blockbuster!   ISBN 1-56280-079-5   10.95

CLAIRE OF THE MOON by Nicole Conn. Audio Book —Read by Marianne Hyatt.   ISBN 1-56280-113-9   16.95

FOR LOVE AND FOR LIFE: INTIMATE PORTRAITS OF LESBIAN COUPLES by Susan Johnson. 224 pp.
                                                                                       ISBN 1-56280-091-4   14.95

DEVOTION by Mindy Kaplan. 192 pp. See the movie — read the book!   ISBN 1-56280-093-0   10.95

SOMEONE TO WATCH by Jaye Maiman. 272 pp. 4th Robin Miller Mystery.   ISBN 1-56280-095-7   10.95

GREENER THAN GRASS by Jennifer Fulton. 208 pp. A young woman — a stranger in her bed.   ISBN 1-56280-092-2   10.95

TRAVELS WITH DIANA HUNTER by Regine Sands. Erotic lesbian romp. Audio Book (2 cassettes)   ISBN 1-56280-107-4   16.95

CABIN FEVER by Carol Schmidt. 256 pp. Sizzling suspense and passion.   ISBN 1-56280-089-1   10.95

THERE WILL BE NO GOODBYES by Laura DeHart Young. 192 pp. Romantic love, strength, and friendship.   ISBN 1-56280-103-1   10.95

FAULTLINE by Sheila Ortiz Taylor. 144 pp. Joyous comic lesbian novel.   ISBN 1-56280-108-2   9.95

OPEN HOUSE by Pat Welch. 176 pp. 4th Helen Black Mystery.   ISBN 1-56280-102-3   10.95

ONCE MORE WITH FEELING by Peggy J. Herring. 240 pp. Lighthearted, loving romantic adventure.   ISBN 1-56280-089-2   11.95

FOREVER by Evelyn Kennedy. 224 pp. Passionate romance — love overcoming all obstacles.   ISBN 1-56280-094-9   10.95

WHISPERS by Kris Bruyer. 176 pp. Romantic ghost story.   ISBN 1-56280-082-5   10.95

NIGHT SONGS by Penny Mickelbury. 224 pp. 2nd Gianna Maglione Mystery.   ISBN 1-56280-097-3   10.95

GETTING TO THE POINT by Teresa Stores. 256 pp. Classic southern Lesbian novel.   ISBN 1-56280-100-7   10.95

PAINTED MOON by Karin Kallmaker. 224 pp. Delicious Kallmaker romance.   ISBN 1-56280-075-2   11.95

THE MYSTERIOUS NAIAD edited by Katherine V. Forrest & Barbara Grier. 320 pp. Love stories by Naiad Press authors.
                                                                                       ISBN 1-56280-074-4   14.95

DAUGHTERS OF A CORAL DAWN by Katherine V. Forrest. 240 pp. Tenth Anniversay Edition.   ISBN 1-56280-104-X   11.95

BODY GUARD by Claire McNab. 208 pp. 6th Carol Ashton
Mystery. ISBN 1-56280-073-6   11.95

CACTUS LOVE by Lee Lynch. 192 pp. Stories by the beloved
storyteller. ISBN 1-56280-071-X   9.95

SECOND GUESS by Rose Beecham. 216 pp. An Amanda
Valentine Mystery. ISBN 1-56280-069-8   9.95

A RAGE OF MAIDENS by Lauren Wright Douglas. 240 pp.
6th Caitlin Reece Mystery. ISBN 1-56280-068-X   10.95

TRIPLE EXPOSURE by Jackie Calhoun. 224 pp. Romantic
drama involving many characters. ISBN 1-56280-067-1   10.95

PERSONAL ADS by Robbi Sommers. 176 pp. Sizzling short
stories. ISBN 1-56280-059-0   11.95

CROSSWORDS by Penny Sumner. 256 pp. 2nd Victoria Cross
Mystery. ISBN 1-56280-064-7   9.95

SWEET CHERRY WINE by Carol Schmidt. 224 pp. A novel of
suspense. ISBN 1-56280-063-9   9.95

CERTAIN SMILES by Dorothy Tell. 160 pp. Erotic short stories.
ISBN 1-56280-066-3   9.95

EDITED OUT by Lisa Haddock. 224 pp. 1st Carmen Ramirez
Mystery. ISBN 1-56280-077-9   9.95

WEDNESDAY NIGHTS by Camarin Grae. 288 pp. Sexy
adventure. ISBN 1-56280-060-4   10.95

SMOKEY O by Celia Cohen. 176 pp. Relationships on the
playing field. ISBN 1-56280-057-4   9.95

KATHLEEN O'DONALD by Penny Hayes. 256 pp. Rose and
Kathleen find each other and employment in 1909 NYC.
ISBN 1-56280-070-1   9.95

STAYING HOME by Elisabeth Nonas. 256 pp. Molly and Alix
want a baby . . . or do they? ISBN 1-56280-076-0   10.95

TRUE LOVE by Jennifer Fulton. 240 pp. Six lesbians searching
for love in all the "right" places. ISBN 1-56280-035-3   11.95

KEEPING SECRETS by Penny Mickelbury. 208 pp. 1st Gianna
Maglione Mystery. ISBN 1-56280-052-3   9.95

THE ROMANTIC NAIAD edited by Katherine V. Forrest &
Barbara Grier. 336 pp. Love stories by Naiad Press authors.
ISBN 1-56280-054-X   14.95

UNDER MY SKIN by Jaye Maiman. 336 pp. 3rd Robin Miller
Mystery. ISBN 1-56280-049-3   11.95

CAR POOL by Karin Kallmaker. 272pp. Lesbians on wheels
and then some! ISBN 1-56280-048-5   10.95

NOT TELLING MOTHER: STORIES FROM A LIFE by Diane
Salvatore. 176 pp. Her 3rd novel. ISBN 1-56280-044-2   9.95

GOBLIN MARKET by Lauren Wright Douglas. 240pp. 5th Caitlin Reece Mystery. ISBN 1-56280-047-7   10.95

FRIENDS AND LOVERS by Jackie Calhoun. 224 pp. Midwestern Lesbian lives and loves. ISBN 1-56280-041-8   11.95

BEHIND CLOSED DOORS by Robbi Sommers. 192 pp. Hot, erotic short stories. ISBN 1-56280-039-6   11.95

CLAIRE OF THE MOON by Nicole Conn. 192 pp. See the movie — read the book! ISBN 1-56280-038-8   11.95

SILENT HEART by Claire McNab. 192 pp. Exotic Lesbian romance. ISBN 1-56280-036-1   11.95

THE SPY IN QUESTION by Amanda Kyle Williams. 256 pp. A Madison McGuire Mystery. ISBN 1-56280-037-X   9.95

SAVING GRACE by Jennifer Fulton. 240 pp. Adventure and romantic entanglement. ISBN 1-56280-051-5   10.95

CURIOUS WINE by Katherine V. Forrest. 176 pp. Tenth Anniversary Edition. The most popular contemporary Lesbian love story.
ISBN 1-56280-053-1   11.95
Audio Book (2 cassettes) ISBN 1-56280-105-8   16.95

CHAUTAUQUA by Catherine Ennis. 192 pp. Exciting, romantic adventure. ISBN 1-56280-032-9   9.95

A PROPER BURIAL by Pat Welch. 192 pp. 3rd Helen Black Mystery. ISBN 1-56280-033-7   9.95

SILVERLAKE HEAT: A Novel of Suspense by Carol Schmidt. 240 pp. Rhonda is as hot as Laney's dreams. ISBN 1-56280-031-0   9.95

LOVE, ZENA BETH by Diane Salvatore. 224 pp. The most talked about lesbian novel of the nineties! ISBN 1-56280-030-2   10.95

A DOORYARD FULL OF FLOWERS by Isabel Miller. 160 pp. Stories incl. 2 sequels to *Patience and Sarah.* ISBN 1-56280-029-9   9.95

MURDER BY TRADITION by Katherine V. Forrest. 288 pp. 4th Kate Delafield Mystery. ISBN 1-56280-002-7   11.95

THE EROTIC NAIAD edited by Katherine V. Forrest & Barbara Grier. 224 pp. Love stories by Naiad Press authors.
ISBN 1-56280-026-4   14.95

DEAD CERTAIN by Claire McNab. 224 pp. 5th Carol Ashton Mystery. ISBN 1-56280-027-2   9.95

CRAZY FOR LOVING by Jaye Maiman. 320 pp. 2nd Robin Miller Mystery. ISBN 1-56280-025-6   10.95

UNCERTAIN COMPANIONS by Robbi Sommers. 204 pp. Steamy, erotic novel. ISBN 1-56280-017-5   11.95

A TIGER'S HEART by Lauren W. Douglas. 240 pp. 4th Caitlin Reece Mystery. ISBN 1-56280-018-3   9.95

PAPERBACK ROMANCE by Karin Kallmaker. 256 pp. A
delicious romance.   ISBN 1-56280-019-1   10.95

THE LAVENDER HOUSE MURDER by Nikki Baker. 224 pp.
2nd Virginia Kelly Mystery.   ISBN 1-56280-012-4   9.95

PASSION BAY by Jennifer Fulton. 224 pp. Passionate romance,
virgin beaches, tropical skies.   ISBN 1-56280-028-0   10.95

STICKS AND STONES by Jackie Calhoun. 208 pp. Contemporary
lesbian lives and loves.   ISBN 1-56280-020-5   9.95
Audio Book (2 cassettes)   ISBN 1-56280-106-6   16.95

UNDER THE SOUTHERN CROSS by Claire McNab. 192 pp.
Romantic nights Down Under.   ISBN 1-56280-011-6   11.95

GRASSY FLATS by Penny Hayes. 256 pp. Lesbian romance in
the '30s.   ISBN 1-56280-010-8   9.95

THE END OF APRIL by Penny Sumner. 240 pp. 1st Victoria
Cross Mystery.   ISBN 1-56280-007-8   8.95

KISS AND TELL by Robbi Sommers. 192 pp. Scorching stories
by the author of *Pleasures*.   ISBN 1-56280-005-1   11.95

STILL WATERS by Pat Welch. 208 pp. 2nd Helen Black Mystery.
                                        ISBN 0-941483-97-5   9.95

TO LOVE AGAIN by Evelyn Kennedy. 208 pp. Wildly romantic
love story.   ISBN 0-941483-85-1   11.95

IN THE GAME by Nikki Baker. 192 pp. 1st Virginia Kelly
Mystery.   ISBN 1-56280-004-3   9.95

STRANDED by Camarin Grae. 320 pp. Entertaining, riveting
adventure.   ISBN 0-941483-99-1   9.95

THE DAUGHTERS OF ARTEMIS by Lauren Wright Douglas.
240 pp. 3rd Caitlin Reece Mystery.   ISBN 0-941483-95-9   9.95

CLEARWATER by Catherine Ennis. 176 pp. Romantic secrets
of a small Louisiana town.   ISBN 0-941483-65-7   8.95

THE HALLELUJAH MURDERS by Dorothy Tell. 176 pp. 2nd
Poppy Dillworth Mystery.   ISBN 0-941483-88-6   8.95

SECOND CHANCE by Jackie Calhoun. 256 pp. Contemporary
Lesbian lives and loves.   ISBN 0-941483-93-2   9.95

BENEDICTION by Diane Salvatore. 272 pp. Striking, contemporary romantic novel.   ISBN 0-941483-90-8   11.95

These are just a few of the many Naiad Press titles — we are the oldest and
largest lesbian/feminist publishing company in the world. We also offer an
enormous selection of lesbian video products. Please request a complete
catalog. We offer personal service; we encourage and welcome direct mail
orders from individuals who have limited access to bookstores carrying our
publications.